# The Prime-Time Crime

"I don't think that camera fell by accident," Joe said.

"So why don't we check out the catwalks?" Frank suggested, bounding up the stairs.

Frank and Joe walked slowly over the maze of narrow platforms extending out into the open space above the studio where the camera had just crashed.

"Here," Frank said, pointing downward. "Footprints in the dust. They look fresh."

The Hardys followed the prints, which suddenly veered to one side of the catwalk. Joe bent over the railing and looked down. "Whoever caused the camera to fall was standing—"

Joe was cut off by the sound of approaching footsteps. A figure wearing a stocking over his face rushed toward Joe and pushed him over the railing. Joe gasped and tumbled over—falling headfirst toward the studio floor thirty feet below!

# The Hardy Boys Mystery Stories

## Available from MINSTREL Books

109

*The*
# HARDY BOYS®

## THE PRIME-
## TIME CRIME

### FRANKLIN W. DIXON

A MINSTREL® BOOK

PUBLISHED BY POCKET BOOKS

New York   London   Toronto   Sydney   Tokyo   Singapore

This book is a work of fiction. Names, characters, places and incidents are either the product of the author's imagination or are used fictitiously. Any resemblance to actual events or locales or persons, living or dead, is entirely coincidental.

A MINSTREL PAPERBACK *ORIGINAL*

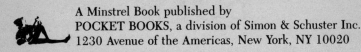

A Minstrel Book published by
POCKET BOOKS, a division of Simon & Schuster Inc.
1230 Avenue of the Americas, New York, NY 10020

Copyright © 1991 by Simon & Schuster Inc.
Cover artwork copyright © 1991 by Paul Bachem
Produced by Mega-Books of New York, Inc.

ISBN: 0-671-69278-X

First Minstrel Books printing August 1991

10  9  8  7  6  5  4  3  2

THE HARDY BOYS MYSTERY STORIES is a trademark of Simon & Schuster

THE HARDY BOYS, A MINSTREL BOOK and colophon are registered trademarks of Simon & Schuster Inc.

Printed in U.S.A.

# Contents

# THE PRIME-
# TIME CRIME

# 1 Where's Clarence?

"Who won the World Series in 1979?" blond-haired Joe Hardy asked his brother, Frank. Joe, a muscular seventeen-year-old, sat his six-foot frame on the edge of a gray couch and stared at his brother through narrowed blue eyes.

"Just give me a second," Frank said, running a hand through his dark hair. "I know this one."

Joe smiled. He was enjoying the fact that he knew the answer to the question without having to look it up in the book he was using to test his brother. Frank, who was a year older and an inch taller than Joe, prided himself on having a great memory for sports facts. But this time, Joe was sure he had him stumped.

1

"Come on," Joe said impatiently. "You're only going to have a few seconds to answer each question when you're on the air. And since you're one-third of the Bayport High School team for 'The Four O'Clock Scholar,' you'd better get at least one-third of the questions right—or we'll lose the contest to Littonville High!"

"Okay, okay," Frank said. "It was . . . um . . . the Philadelphia Phillies."

"Wrong," Joe said, pounding his fist on the arm of the couch. "The Pittsburgh Pirates."

"Oh, right," Frank said in a disgruntled tone. "The Phillies won the 1980 World Series. I always get those two games mixed up. Next question."

Just then, a voice behind the Hardys said, "Hey, what's with all these sports questions?"

Joe turned to see Steve Burke, a classmate from Bayport High School, settle himself on the arm of the sofa. Steve, who was one of Frank's teammates on the daily quiz show, was tall and gangly, with tightly curled red hair and a freckled face. He wore a loose-fitting T-shirt with the slogan Genius on Board printed on it. The three teenagers—Frank, Joe, and Steve—were gathered in a sparsely furnished room with a sign on the wall that read WBPT greenroom. Taped to the sign was a piece of paper on which was written " 'Four O'Clock Scholar' contestants must be in the greenroom by 3:30." In the opposite corner of the room were the three team members from Bayport's rival, Littonville High.

2

"They always ask sports questions on 'The Four O'Clock Scholar,'" Joe said to Steve.

"Yeah," Steve replied. "But they also ask questions on science, history, and current events."

"Not to mention art, literature, and music," added Debbie Hertzberg, the third member of the Bayport team. She had stepped into the room and was standing behind Steve. Debbie had brown eyes and long black hair that hung down below her shoulders. She wore a blue dress with a high neck and flat black shoes.

"Unfortunately," Frank said, "the sports questions are the only ones my brother knows the answers to."

"We had to know about lots of subjects to get on this show," Debbie said, looking sideways at Joe. "Not just sports trivia."

"Okay, okay," Joe said. He held up the fact book, which was entitled *Everything You Always Wanted to Know About Everything.* "From now on I'll only ask you questions from this book."

"I bet I can answer them before Frank does," Steve proclaimed, a gleam in his eyes.

"And I bet I can answer them before *you* do," Debbie said to Steve.

"You?" Steve said. "Sorry, Deb! Everybody knows I'm smarter than you are."

"Then everybody's wrong," Debbie retorted.

"Look, guys," Joe said with a sigh. "The quiz starts in fifteen minutes. Just let me ask you a couple of questions before they chase me out of here."

"Fire away," Steve said.

Joe flipped through the pages of the book. "Here's a good one," he said. "Which of the nine planets of the solar system has the longest day?"

"Mercury," Steve declared. "Because it's the closest to the sun, and the sun's gravity slows it down."

"No. It's Jupiter," Debbie insisted. "Because it's the biggest planet and takes the longest to complete its rotation."

"Frank?" Joe asked. "Can you come up with the right answer?" He glanced at Steve and Debbie, who were both looking skeptically at Frank.

"Well," Frank said, "actually, I thought it was Venus."

"Bingo," Joe said. "That's the correct answer."

"What!" Steve shouted, trying to grab the book out of Joe's hands. "Give me that book. What kind of stupid answer is that?"

"The right one," Joe said, holding the book out of Steve's reach. "Which didn't happen to be the one you—or Debbie—gave."

"Lucky guess," Debbie said. "Why don't you ask a question about art or literature? I always do better on those."

"Art or literature," Joe repeated, flipping through the pages again. "Those are in a different part of the book. Let's see. . . ."

"Excuse me," said a new voice. They all looked toward the door and saw the producer of "The Four

O'Clock Scholar," Marcy Simons, enter the room. Frank and Joe remembered her from the last time they were at the station, working on the case *Danger on the Air*. Marcy was thirty-five years old, with short-cropped black hair and large-framed glasses. She wore a dark gray suit with a white shirt, and she carried a clipboard underneath one arm.

"You'll be going on the air in a few minutes," she said. She looked across the room at the team from Littonville High. "Would the contestants please follow me?" Then she turned to Joe. "Visitors will have to leave now."

"I was just going," Joe said, standing up. He punched Frank lightly on the arm. "Give 'em your best shot, bro."

"I just hope my best shot can hit the broad side of a barn," Frank said.

"Relax, Frank," Steve said. "I've got all the answers. You can just sit back and let me do the work."

"You can both relax," Debbie added. "I'm sure I can handle this all by myself."

"Oh, yeah?" Steve said. "You and what encyclopedia?"

Joe glanced at Steve and Debbie as he walked out of the greenroom and into the hallway. They were starting to get on his nerves. Poor Frank, Joe thought. He's stuck with those two for another hour.

Joe walked to the far end of the hallway and

5

entered WBPT's Studio A. He flashed his admittance pass at the guard who stood by the door. Two sets of bleachers had been set up against one wall of the room, one for students from Bayport High and the other for Littonville students. Joe recognized a number of his friends on the Bayport bleachers.

"Hey, Joe," Chet Morton shouted as Joe approached. "I saved you a seat. Come on up."

"Thanks, Chet," Joe said. He climbed up the steps two at a time and sat next to his husky friend. "I was prepping Frank for the quiz."

"Telling him everything you know, huh?" Chet said between gulps of the ham-and-cheese sandwich he was eating. "What did you do during the next thirty seconds?"

"Very funny," Joe said. "Hey, are you allowed to bring food into the studio?"

"Nobody told me I couldn't," Chet retorted. "I was getting awfully hungry waiting for the show to start. Which reminds me . . ." The dark-haired teen reached into his knapsack and pulled out a bag of potato chips.

Joe grinned. "Think that will last you until the show's ended?"

"Give me a break," Chet protested. "Football season's over and I'm not in training right now."

An attractive girl with a thick mane of brown hair slid into the seat next to Joe. "You're going to say hello, aren't you?" Iola Morton said. Iola was Chet's sister and Joe's girlfriend.

6

"Hey there," said a blond girl who sat down next to Iola. "You're not going to get stuck up just because your brother—and my boyfriend—is a contestant on 'The Four O'Clock Scholar,' are you?" Callie Shaw gave Joe a mock frown.

"Sorry, Callie, Iola," Joe said with a wide grin. "I was just checking in with Chet. You guys ready for the show?"

"Definitely," Iola said. "We've been getting ready all week. Look at the sign we made."

Iola and Callie held up a five-foot-long painted banner that read "Bayport High is number one, and so is Frank Hardy!"

"How do you like it?" Iola asked.

"It's great," Joe said. "But I don't know how much Steve and Debbie are going to like it. They both think they're number one."

"I know," Callie replied. "I hope they remember that they're part of a team."

"I can't wait to see Clarence Kellerman hosting the show," Chet said. "I hear he comes out before the show and does a comedy routine to get the audience warmed up."

"I heard that, too!" Iola said excitedly. "Clarence is one of my favorite TV stars."

"Actually, he should be out here already," Joe said, looking at his watch. "I wonder where he is."

"He's probably backstage warming up for his entrance," Chet said.

"I love that part," Callie said. "Where he comes

7

cartwheeling out from backstage, lands on his feet, and says, 'Hey, everybody! It's your old buddy Clarence!' "

"Here comes somebody now," Chet said, nodding toward the set.

Joe turned toward the set and saw Marcy Simons step from behind a light gray curtain. Following her were the teams of students from Bayport and Littonville. Joe smiled when he saw that someone, probably Marcy, had slipped a sports jacket over Steve's T-shirt. Steve didn't look very happy about it.

"There's Frank!" Callie said.

"And Steve and Debbie," Iola added.

"My favorite people," Joe muttered.

Joe noticed two long tables on the set, one labeled Bayport, the other Littonville. Behind each table were three microphones and three chairs. Marcy Simons led Frank, Steve, and Debbie to one table and the Littonville team to the other.

As a stagehand showed the team members how to use the electronic equipment on the table, Marcy strode over to a man wearing a headset with a microphone attached. She talked to him quickly and urgently.

Joe watched her as she talked. There was a worried look on her face, and she seemed nervous.

"We want to see Clarence!" somebody shouted from the back of the bleachers.

"Yeah!" another fan shouted. "Where's Clarence?"

Someone behind Joe began to chant, "Clarence, Clarence!" The other members of the audience joined in, shouting Clarence's name over and over, just as the audience always did at the beginning of "The Four O'Clock Scholar."

Marcy Simons looked toward the audience and frowned, then turned back to the man with the headset. He spoke briefly into his microphone, then said something to Marcy.

The producer faced the audience and waved her hands crosswise in front of her.

"Quiet!" she yelled, loudly enough so that she could be heard over the repeated chanting of Clarence's name. The audience fell silent. Then Marcy said to the man with the microphone, "Tell them to keep rolling commercials. We'll start the show when I tell them to start the show."

"Right," said the man with the headset, repeating into his microphone what the producer had said.

"What's happening?" Iola whispered to her friends.

"Yeah," Chet said. "Where's our old buddy Clarence?"

"You got me," Joe said with a shrug.

Marcy Simons looked at the audience, an angry expression on her face. "I'll tell you where your old buddy Clarence is. He's missing. And this show is scheduled to go on the air live in five seconds— whether he's here or not!"

# 2 Way to Go, Frank!

Joe Hardy stood up in his seat, startled. "Clarence?" he asked. "Missing? You mean he just didn't show up for work today?"

"That's exactly what I mean," Marcy said shortly.

Several people in the audience groaned with disappointment.

"But that's impossible," Chet said. "Clarence has never missed a show in seventeen years. Everybody knows that. Something must have happened to him."

"Something is *going* to happen to that clown when I get my hands on him," Marcy snapped. "And if I don't find a substitute host in a hurry, we'll have a half hour of dead air on our hands. We can't run commercials forever."

Just then the man with the headset spun around and faced Marcy. "Matt Freeman is in Studio B!" he cried. "He can be here in five minutes."

"He'd better be here in one minute," Marcy told the man. She raced toward the studio door.

Joe looked at his watch. "Freeman better get here soon. This is serious."

A few seconds later, Marcy reappeared with a middle-aged man in tow.

"There he is," Joe said to his friends. "That's Freeman."

"Doesn't Freeman host that afternoon talk show, 'Faces and Places'?" Iola asked.

"That's right," Callie said. "You and Frank were on that show once, weren't you, Joe?"

Joe nodded. "Somebody set off a bomb in the studio while we were there."

"Oh, great," Chet said nervously. "I hope that doesn't happen today."

Joe turned away from his friends and focused his attention on the set. Matt Freeman was a handsome man with a tanned face and black hair peppered with gray. He wore a dark suit with a blue tie that he was hastily tightening around his neck. Marcy pushed him behind the podium that stood between the two long tables.

"You've seen the show, right?" she asked him, thrusting a sheet of paper into his hands before he could answer. "Here are the questions. All you have to do is ask them. I'll signal you when it's time for a commercial break."

11

As Matt clipped a microphone on his jacket, Marcy raced off the set, waving at the camera operators. "Set up the opening shot. Fast. We're on the air in fifteen seconds."

The crew swung the cameras into position. One was aimed toward Matt Freeman, a second toward Frank and his two teammates, and a third pulled out for a full shot of the host and the two teams. Joe looked at a video monitor on one side of the set. An advertisement for a fast-food restaurant was just ending. It was replaced by a shot of "The Four O'Clock Scholar" set, with the name of the show superimposed over it in green letters.

Matt Freeman smiled at the camera while the theme song played. Joe noticed how comfortable Freeman appeared. It looked as though he had been hosting the show all his life.

"Good afternoon, everybody," he said genially. "And welcome to 'The Four O'Clock Scholar,' everyone's favorite Sunday afternoon quiz show. I'm afraid your old buddy Clarence couldn't be here today. I'm Matt Freeman, and I'll be standing in for Clarence. We've got two great high school teams for you today, from two of my favorite schools—" He darted a sidelong glance toward the banners that had been draped across the fronts of the tables. "Bayport High and Littonville High, of course."

"This is going to be some show," Chet whispered. "He doesn't even know the names of the schools."

"Give him a break," Joe whispered back. "He just got here."

"Now let me introduce our young contestants," Freeman said, walking toward the two teams. Reading the names off the nameplates in front of the three students, he said, "For Bayport High, we have Frank Hardy, Steve Burke, and Debbie Hertzberg."

The Bayport students in the audience clapped wildly at the mention of each name. Joe and his friends cheered loudly when Frank's name was mentioned. Freeman then read off the names of the three students from Littonville High, and the quiz began.

"I'm sure you all know the rules," Freeman said. "I ask the question, and the first student to press the buzzer at his or her seat gets to answer. If the student who rings the buzzer doesn't know the answer, any other member of the team can respond. And if nobody on the team knows the answer, the point goes to the other team.

"Ready? Okay, let's begin."

Frank sat up alertly in his chair. Freeman stepped back behind his podium and read the first question.

"Many people regard Albert Einstein as the greatest scientist of the twentieth century and perhaps the greatest scientist of all time," read Freeman. "In his most famous equation, $E$ equals $MC$ squared, the $E$ stands for 'energy' and the $C$ stands for the 'speed of light.' What does the letter $M$ stand for?"

Steve stabbed at his buzzer so hard that the table shook. "Matter!" he shouted loudly.

"Wrong," Freeman replied. "Does anyone else on the Bayport team know the answer?"

Joe saw Debbie shoot Freeman a bored look, as if to say, "That's not my kind of question."

Frank leaned forward and said, "Mass."

"Correct," Freeman said. "The complete equation says that 'energy equals mass times the speed of light squared.' That's ten points to the Bayport team."

Steve turned to Frank and mouthed the words, "I knew that."

"Many of the short stories of Ernest Hemingway," Freeman continued, reading from the paper in front of him, "including his famous story 'The Killers,' were concerned with the adventures of a young man who literary critics believe represents Hemingway himself when he was growing up. What was the name of the young man?"

"I love Hemingway!" Debbie cried, pushing down on her buzzer. "I've read all his stories. The young man was named, uh, he was named—I know the answer, honest."

"I'm sorry, but your five seconds are up," Freeman announced. "Would anyone else like to try?"

"It was Nick Adams," Frank offered.

"You're absolutely right, Frank," Freeman said. "Another ten points for the Bayport team."

The Bayport half of the audience clapped and cheered loudly.

14

"Wow," Chet said, turning to Joe. "I didn't know Frank knew all this stuff."

"My own brother," Joe said, joking. "Hard to believe."

"Frank really is very smart," Callie said proudly. "He's got brains and he's a great athlete."

"True," said Joe with a sly grin. "Actually, he's not that great at baseball."

Iola rolled her eyes. "Right, Joe," she said with a chuckle. "We all know that you're the baseball king."

"Sssh," Callie whispered. "Freeman's going to ask the next question."

"Every Memorial Day, millions of automobile racing fans stay home, glued to their television screens for the running of the classic Indianapolis Five Hundred race," the emcee continued. "In what year was the first Indy Five Hundred held?"

This time it was Frank who rang his buzzer first. Steve and Debbie turned to him with slightly annoyed looks on their faces.

"In 1911?" Frank asked.

"That's right," Freeman announced. "The Bayport team does it again, and it looks like Frank Hardy is leading the way."

"Way to go, Frank!" Joe shouted at the top of his lungs.

"Yay, Bayport!" came the cheers from the others in the Bayport half of the bleachers. "Yay, Frank!"

"This is so exciting," Callie said. "I knew Frank could do it."

15

"Hey, look," Iola said, pointing at a studio monitor. "We're on TV."

Joe turned and looked at the screen. Sure enough, the camera was aimed directly at them, and their beaming faces were filling the screen.

"Hi, Mom," Joe said, waving at the camera. "Hi, Dad."

"Send money," Chet added. "And food."

"And now for the next question," Matt Freeman said. He rattled off several questions, many of which Frank was able to answer. The Littonville High team also managed a few answers, but Steve and Debbie sat glumly, rarely ringing their buzzers.

During the first commercial, Frank leaned back in his seat. His heart was racing. He was exhilarated over how well he had done in the first round, though he was also aware that Steve and Debbie were glaring at him from the other two seats.

Frank looked up to see Marcy Simons dart out onto the set. She ran around nervously, congratulating Matt Freeman on his performance, praising the two teams for their fast thinking, and handing Freeman the new set of questions for the second round.

When the commercial was over, Freeman fired off another series of questions. Although Steve and Debbie managed to score a few points, Frank still found himself giving most of the correct answers. By the end of the game, the Littonville team was hopelessly behind, and Frank's team scored an easy victory.

16

"Let's hear it for the Bayport team!" shouted Matt Freeman, but the Bayport half of the audience didn't need his encouragement. They were already on their feet, clapping, whistling, and shouting Frank's name. Joe and Chet were the loudest.

"And I want to remind all of you," Freeman said when the cheering had died down, "that our championship tournament will begin this Tuesday on a special edition of 'The Four O'Clock Scholar.' The Bayport High team will be back to square off against our current reigning champion, Newcastle High School. We'll all be looking forward to seeing Frank, Debbie, and Steve again on Tuesday night."

Freeman waved at the camera, and the credits began to roll. As soon as the show was over, Frank joined his brother and his friends.

"Hey, Frank," Chet said, slapping him on the back. "Good work. I didn't know you were *that* smart."

"I did," Joe said proudly.

"Me, too," Callie said with a broad smile. Iola nodded and grinned.

Steve Burke walked up to Frank and extended his hand. "Congratulations, Hardy," he said glumly. "You had a run of luck back there."

"Hey," Joe said. "That wasn't luck, it was brilliance. My brother's a genius. It runs in the family."

Frank gave Joe a funny look. "You've never called me that before."

"Shut up, stupid," Joe said, grinning. "I can call you a genius if I want to."

17

Marcy Simons, who had been in a conversation with Matt Freeman, turned to the remaining members of the audience.

"I'm afraid you'll have to leave now," she told them. "The show's over, and we need the studio for another program."

"What happened to Clarence?" Chet asked. "Did you ever find him?"

"Not yet," Marcy said. "But we're looking, believe me." She started to turn away, then did a double take at the sight of Joe and Frank. "Hey, haven't I seen you two before?"

"We're Joe and Frank Hardy," Joe said. "We've lived in Bayport all our lives."

"I know," Marcy said, snapping her fingers. "You're the detectives who helped catch the Masked Marauder a while back, the guy who was threatening to blow up the station."

"Right," Frank said. "In fact, he almost did blow up the studio, while we were appearing on the show 'Faces and Places.'"

Marcy looked at the Hardys thoughtfully. "That was an impressive piece of detective work," she said. "I'd like to talk with you two—alone."

"Well, we can take a hint," Callie said. "Come on, Iola. Let's meet the rest of the gang over at Mr. Pizza."

"Now you're talking," Chet said, a big grin spreading across his face. "I haven't had a square meal in, oh, three or four hours."

18

"What about the sandwich and those chips you ate before the show?" Joe asked.

"That was just a snack," Chet answered.

"Do you two want to come along?" Iola asked Steve and Debbie.

"Not right now," Debbie said. She was still a little upset over her poor performance on the show. "I'll catch up with you later."

"Likewise," Steve said.

When everyone had left the studio, Joe turned to Marcy Simons. "So what was it you wanted to talk to us about? Does it have something to do with Clarence?"

"Yes," Marcy said. "I'd like you two to do a little detective work for us."

"Sure," Frank said. "We're always happy to help out."

"Do you really think that something has happened to Clarence?" Joe asked. "Maybe he just had a flat tire."

"I'm afraid there's a little more to it than that," Marcy said, pulling a sheet of paper from the clipboard under her arm. "This was delivered by a messenger, just after the show started."

Joe took the paper from Marcy. It was a sheet of white paper with a typewritten message on it. The paper was folded in two. Joe read it out loud.

" 'Marcy— Going away for a two-week vacation. Sorry I couldn't tell you in advance. Hope you can find somebody to fill in for me.' " Looking up at his brother, Joe said, "It's signed by Clarence Kellerman."

"Is that Clarence's signature?" Frank asked.

"Yes, it is," Marcy replied.

"Then what's the problem?" Joe asked. "It looks like Clarence just skipped town for a few days."

"Open it up and look inside," Marcy said.

Joe opened the folded sheet of paper. Inside, handwritten in large, jagged letters, was a single word: HELP.

# 3 Too Many Detectives

"Wow!" Joe exclaimed, staring at the note. "This definitely changes things."

"Did you talk to the messenger?" Frank asked. "Did he say where he got this?"

Marcy nodded. "The messenger service received a call telling them to pick up the message at a convenience store in the middle of town that recently went out of business. When the messenger got there, he found the message taped to the door, with the money for the delivery attached to it with a paper clip. He has no idea who put it there."

"It looks like somebody typed the message, then forced Clarence to sign it," Joe said. "The typist didn't notice that Clarence had written a message of his own on it."

"Have you called the police?" Frank asked Marcy. "If this is a kidnapping, they should be involved."

"The police are already investigating," Marcy said. "I called them during the show, and I've got to go talk with them now. But I was impressed by the detective work you two did during the last case, and I'd like to buy a little insurance by having you two around."

"We'd be glad to help," Frank said.

"Do you know when Clarence was last seen?" Joe asked.

"The receptionist at the front desk saw him arrive just before nine o'clock this morning, but nobody's seen him since," Marcy said.

"Then he could still be in the building," Frank said.

"That's possible," Marcy said. "Believe me, I've got people looking for him. And I've arranged for guards to be placed at all of the doors twenty-four hours a day, in case he tries to leave."

"Voluntarily or involuntarily," Joe added.

"Right," Marcy said. "I'm asking the two of you to help because I think this is a very serious situation. If Clarence has been kidnapped, he could be in a lot of danger."

"Did I hear you say that Clarence has been kidnapped?" asked Steve Burke, who had just stepped into the studio. He stopped and looked at the Hardys and Marcy with interest.

"It's nothing, Steve," Joe said casually. "I thought you were heading over to Mr. Pizza."

"I'll be going over there in a few minutes," Steve said. "Hey, what's that?" Steve looked at the paper in Joe's hand. "A ransom note?"

Before Joe could stop him, Steve grabbed the note out of his hand. "Hey! A note from Clarence," Steve said. "And it's got the word *help* in big letters inside. It looks like our old buddy Clarence really has been kidnapped!"

"Give me that note, young man," Marcy said, holding out her hand. Sheepishly, Steve handed the paper back to her. "This information is not to leave this building," she warned. "Do you understand? Clarence Kellerman is apparently in a great deal of trouble, and it won't help him or the station to announce the fact all over Bayport."

"Sorry," Steve said. "But won't this be in the newspapers tomorrow?"

"Not if we can help it," Marcy said. "With any luck, Clarence will be back safe and sound by tomorrow, perhaps with the help of your friends here."

"These guys?" Steve said with a laugh. "Ha! They couldn't find a wrench at a plumber's convention. I bet I could find Clarence faster than they could."

"What do you mean by—" Joe began.

Suddenly Debbie Hertzberg appeared from the hallway outside the studio. "Have you found Clarence yet?" she asked Marcy. "I figured he just got held up on the way to the station."

"Wrong," Steve said. "He's been kidnapped."

"Kidnapped?" Debbie said with a gasp. "That's incredible!"

"Look, do you think maybe we could keep this a secret?" Joe suggested. "Just between the five of us—and anyone else within hearing range?" he added sarcastically.

Marcy flashed the four teenagers an exasperated look. "I'll be down the hall in my office, talking to the police, if you need more details," she told them. Clutching her clipboard tightly under her arm, she left the studio.

"Marcy doesn't look too happy," Joe said. "She only asked us to take the case a few minutes ago. I hope she doesn't change her mind."

"No loss," Steve said with a shrug. "I can take on the case."

"Oh yeah?" Joe said, raising his eyebrows. "I suppose you could do better?"

"Absolutely," Steve said. "In fact, I bet I solve this Clarence Kellerman case before you guys do."

Joe rolled his eyes. "Give me a break. What do you know about detective work?"

"I plan to be a scientist one day," Steve said. "All scientists are detectives. We sift through clues to get answers. I'll find the identity of Clarence Kellerman's kidnapper just like Einstein found that energy equals matter times the speed of light squared."

"That's *mass* times the speed of light squared," Frank reminded him.

"Whatever," Steve said. "This case sounds like it ought to be a piece of cake for me."

"Okay, Einstein," Joe said. "You're on. We'll see if you can solve this case faster than we can."

"Well," Frank said, "I suppose it couldn't hurt. And if it means Clarence is found even sooner, all the better."

"What about me?" Debbie asked. "I've read hundreds of mystery novels. I think I know a thing or two about being a detective."

"Hang it up, Debbie," Steve said. "Leave the detective work to the real brains, like me."

"You mean the pea brains like you, don't you?" Debbie replied hotly.

"Let's keep this civilized," Frank said. "If you two want to prove that you're great detectives, that's okay, but you don't have to fight over it."

"There's no need to fight," Steve said. "I'll find Clarence first using sheer brainpower. In fact, he's practically as good as found."

"If anyone finds Clarence first," Debbie said, "it'll be me. I'll bet that there are clues to his disappearance all over this station. And with my refined powers of observation, I'll find them right away."

"Great," Frank said. "Now let's get started."

"Right," Steve said. "I want to get this investigation underway as soon as possible. Come on, Deb.

Let's show these two amateurs how real detectives solve a case."

"Sorry, Steve," Debbie said, sauntering toward the door of the studio. "I work alone. You're on your own."

As soon as Steve and Debbie were gone, Joe turned and stared at his brother. "I think we've created a couple of monsters," he said.

"Oh, I don't think they can hurt anything," Frank replied, chuckling. "And, who knows, maybe they'll actually find Clarence."

"It's more likely they'll get bored and quit after an hour or two," Joe said. "It won't take long before they learn how tough detective work really is."

"Speaking of detective work," Frank said, "we'd better start doing some ourselves. Where do you want to start?"

"I think we should talk to Marcy Simons again," Joe said. "We need to find out what's been going on around the station since the last time we were here."

"Sounds good," Frank said. "Let's go. I think I remember where her office is."

Marcy Simons's small office was in the hallway not far from Studio A. Frank knocked on the door. The producer opened the door and nodded when she saw the Hardys.

"You just missed the police," she said. "I told them what happened, and they said they'd keep an eye out for Clarence, but they weren't sure there was much they could do."

26

"We were wondering how things have been around the station since we were here last," Frank said. He and his brother took seats as Marcy settled down behind her desk. "Is Bill Amberson still the station manager?"

Marcy shook her head. "He decided to take an early retirement and move to Arizona. His family sold the station to the Mediagenic Corporation."

"So who's the new station manager?" Joe asked.

"Ted Whalen," Marcy replied. Frank noticed the slightly annoyed tone in her voice as she pronounced his name. "Fresh out of college and already a vice president at Mediagenic. Comes from a wealthy old New England family."

"Sounds like you don't like him much," Frank said.

Marcy smiled. "Did I say that? I guess I just miss Bill. Once in a while he could be a little grumpy, but he had a big heart. Ted Whalen's a little hard to warm up to."

"Why don't you introduce us to him?" Joe asked. "Maybe he can give us some clue as to what happened to Clarence."

"Sure," Marcy said. "It couldn't hurt."

As Marcy led the Hardys into the hallway, Frank heard loud voices coming from Studio A.

"I found a clue," declared a female voice. "Hey, let go of that."

"It's mine!" shouted a male voice. "I found it first."

"What in the world is going on in there?" Marcy asked.

The Hardys looked at each other. "I think I've got a pretty good idea," Frank said.

The brothers hurried over to the studio. As they entered the room, they saw Steve and Debbie fighting over a man's gray suit jacket. Steve had a grip on one sleeve, Debbie the other, and the fabric was on the verge of tearing down the middle.

"You're trying to take this away from me so I can't solve the case," Debbie said.

"Oh yeah?" Steve shouted. "That's exactly what you're doing."

Frank stepped over to them. "There's not going to be much evidence left if you two rip that jacket apart," he said.

"I found this piece of evidence first," Steve insisted.

"Listen, you two," Frank began, placing a hand on Steve's shoulder. Suddenly Frank heard a sound from above. Startled, he looked up. Near the studio ceiling, a huge television camera, at the end of the long boom that supported it, was swaying and starting to break loose from its moorings. As Frank watched, it snapped free.

The camera was about to fall right on top of Steve, Debbie, and Frank.

# 4 Intruder in the Shadows

"Look out!" Frank yelled, grabbing Steve under his arms and yanking him out of the way of the falling camera.

"Hey!" Steve shouted as he let go of the jacket. He tried to struggle out of Frank's grip, but succeeded only in tumbling both of them to the floor.

"What?" Debbie said in astonishment as Joe shot forward, grabbed her squarely around the waist, and pushed her sideways into a painted wooden flat just as the camera crashed to the floor. The flat they collided with fell to the ground at almost the same instant, with Joe and Debbie on top of it.

"What are you doing?" Debbie shouted. "You let go of me. You won't get your hands on my evidence that easily." She clutched the jacket tightly.

"I was trying to help you," Joe muttered.

"Go easy on my brother," Frank said, as he got to his feet. "He just saved your life."

"What are you talking—" Debbie stopped in midsentence as she noticed the smashed remains of the camera lying on the floor. "Oh, no! Where did that come from?"

"From up there," Frank said, pointing to the ceiling. "If Joe and I hadn't gotten you two out of the way in a hurry, you'd have the world's worst headaches right about now."

Steve rose unsteadily to his feet. "You mean that thing almost fell on us?"

"That's about the size of it," Joe said as he extracted himself and Debbie from the battered flat. "And I'm not convinced it was an accident."

Debbie's eyes widened. "Are you saying that somebody tried to kill us?" she asked in disbelief.

"This must be a really valuable piece of evidence," Steve said, grabbing the jacket from Debbie, who had relaxed her grip on it. "Somebody's willing to kill us for it. Boy, am I glad I found it."

"Give that back to me," Debbie demanded. "I found that piece of evidence."

Frank grabbed the jacket away from Steve. "This case will get solved a lot faster if we share the evidence. For all we know, Clarence Kellerman's life may be at stake. It's irresponsible to risk his life just for the sake of proving which of us is the better detective."

Steve looked sheepish. "You're right. I'm sorry."

Debbie started to reply angrily, then thought better of it. "I guess that makes sense. Okay, we'll share the evidence."

"Good," Frank said. "Now what is this thing, anyway?"

"It's a man's jacket," Steve said.

"I can see that," Frank said. "But why is it evidence?"

"I found it next to the set of 'The Four O'Clock Scholar,'" Debbie said.

"I found it," Steve interrupted.

"No squabbling, remember?" Frank said, holding up his hand in warning.

"We both found it," Debbie said reluctantly. "And we think it must have been left here by Clarence Kellerman."

"Why do you think that?" Joe asked.

"Because," Steve said hesitantly, "it's a man's jacket and, well, Clarence is a man."

"What a clever connection," Joe said. "I never would have thought of it."

Marcy rushed into the studio. "I heard a crash," she said, then stopped when she saw the smashed camera. "What happened here?"

Frank explained, then asked the producer about the jacket.

"That jacket belongs to Matt Freeman," Marcy told them. "He always keeps a spare in the studio in case something happens to the one he's wearing. He has a habit of spilling coffee on his jacket."

Frank looked at the wrinkled, dust-stained jacket. "I'm afraid he'll have to get this one dry-cleaned. Actually, he's lucky he doesn't have to buy a new one," he added with a glance at Steve and Debbie.

Marcy took the jacket from Frank. "I want to apologize for what happened with that camera," she said. "I don't know what could have gone wrong. The camera crews are usually careful to make sure that everything is secure and in place."

"Maybe Joe's right," Frank said, looking at his brother. "Maybe it wasn't an accident."

Debbie looked stunned. "That means somebody really might have been trying to kill us."

"It's possible," Frank said. "Whoever's responsible for Clarence's disappearance may be a desperate person. I hope this makes you think twice about playing detective."

"Are you implying that I might give up?" Debbie asked.

"Look," Joe said. "This isn't a detective novel. Things could get really dangerous from here on out. Kidnapping is serious business."

"Well, I still plan to solve this case," Debbie said firmly. "If Clarence Kellerman's life is in danger, then he needs my help more than ever."

"Is that my jacket?" said a man's voice from the doorway. "It looks like somebody tried to iron it with their feet."

The Hardys turned to see Matt Freeman step into the studio.

32

"Oh, hello, Matt," Marcy said. "Sorry about the jacket. We had a little, ah, accident."

"So I see," Matt said, looking at the smashed pieces of the fallen camera as he took the jacket from Marcy. "What happened there? Looks pretty nasty. Was my jacket underneath that when it fell?"

"Not exactly," Marcy said, looking eager to change the subject. "You remember the Hardys, don't you, Matt?"

"Of course," he said, stepping forward with a smile and offering his hand for Frank and Joe to shake. "You did a great job on the show this afternoon, Frank."

"Thanks, Matt," Frank said. "You haven't heard anything from Clarence since then, have you?"

"Not yet," Matt said, "but he'll turn up. He's just grandstanding again. Clarence likes pulling silly publicity stunts."

"Come on, Matt," Marcy said. "You don't think Clarence would vanish like this just to get attention, do you?"

"Why not?" Matt said with a shrug. "Remember that time he pretended to break his leg when he fell off the edge of the set, then took the cast off in the middle of the show a week later and danced around the studio? We got angry phone calls all day from people who had sent sympathy cards thinking he was really hurt."

"That's not the same thing," Marcy insisted.

"Maybe not," Matt said, "but I bet Clarence turns up safe and sound during Tuesday night's

33

show. He'll probably pop out from backstage and announce, 'Your old buddy Clarence is back!' "

"If he does," Marcy said, "Ted Whalen'll fire him so fast his head will spin."

"That's a pleasant thought," Matt said, a gleam in his eye.

"You sound like you'd be happy if Clarence got fired," Frank said.

"Not me. I love the guy," Matt replied. Frank could tell that Matt was being sarcastic. "And I certainly wouldn't want anything to happen to the host of Bayport's longest-running TV show," Matt went on. "Why, he's an institution in this town."

"That's right," Marcy said.

"Listen, you guys," Matt said, "I've got to get moving. Got a hot date at the dry cleaner's to get my jacket pressed."

"Sorry about the damage to your suit, Mr. Freeman," Debbie said.

"No problem," Matt said. "I get a special discount at the cleaner's. They're great at taking out coffee stains, and I doubt that this will give them much trouble."

"I'm leaving, too," Steve said, after Freeman had left. "Got to find more clues to Clarence's whereabouts."

"You don't think Matt Freeman's right about Clarence pulling a publicity stunt?" Debbie asked, following Steve to the door.

"I don't know." Steve shrugged. "Even if he is, there's still a mystery to solve, right? If I can find

Clarence before he pops out from behind the curtain Tuesday night, it still proves what a great detective I am."

"True. But that's not going to happen. I'll be the one to find him first," Debbie said as the door shut behind her.

Frank and Joe stared after them in exasperation.

"Where'd you find that pair?" Marcy asked with a frown.

"They found us," Frank said. "Now we can't get rid of them."

"Weren't you going to introduce us to the new station manager?" Joe reminded Marcy.

"Oh, right," Marcy said. "Come on. His office is upstairs."

Marcy led the Hardys out of the studio and up a flight of stairs to a luxurious suite of offices on the second floor. Frank looked around at the expensively framed paintings that hung on the wall, and the thick pile carpeting that lined the hallway.

"Somebody's been redecorating," he commented to Marcy. "These offices didn't look this nice the last time Joe and I were here."

"Mediagenic's pumping a lot of money into the station," Marcy explained. "They have big plans. They want to turn it into a showcase."

When they arrived at Ted Whalen's office, the door was open. Whalen held up a finger to tell Marcy he'd be with her in a moment.

Frank was impressed with the size of the office. It was at least fifty feet deep and just as wide, with sleek, ultra-modern furniture set on a lush blue carpet. On one wall were ten television monitors, simultaneously showing an array of network and cable programs. Whalen sat behind a large desk, leaning back in a leather chair as he chatted on the telephone. He was a blond, slender young man who looked to be in his mid-twenties. He was wearing an expensive-looking tailored suit.

"Busy guy," Frank whispered. "Must be talking with a producer or something."

"Probably talking with an accountant," Marcy whispered back. "Ted cares a lot more about how much money the programs make than about what actually goes into them."

After a few minutes Whalen hung up the phone and turned to his guests. "Good to see you, Marcy," he said in a clipped tone, without smiling. "What brings you up here at five-thirty? Working late, I see. I admire that."

"Thanks, Ted," Marcy said. "I just wanted to introduce you to Frank and Joe Hardy. They're young detectives who've helped out here at the station before. I've asked them to assist us in finding Clarence Kellerman."

"Oh, yes, Kellerman," Whalen said, without changing expression. "Terrible thing. I heard about the note you found. Pity if something happens to one of our best talent properties."

"I'm glad to hear you say that," Marcy said. "I'd heard a rumor that you were thinking of canceling Clarence's show."

"It's under consideration," Whalen said, nodding. "Clarence is popular, but the audience on 'Scholar' is a bit old for my taste. I've found that it's mostly the parents of students who watch the show, not the students themselves. I'm sure we can find a role for Clarence, though. Perhaps he could host a music video show. There's a nationally syndicated news magazine show we'd like to put in the 'Scholar' slot. Less production expense, more profit."

"I watch 'Scholar' every week," Frank said. "So do all my friends."

"Then you hang out with an unusual crowd," Whalen said coldly. He pointed to a thick stack of folders on his desk. "I have reports here from the best research firms in the country telling me who watches what, and 'Scholar' just isn't cutting it with the youth market."

"Do you have any idea what happened to Clarence, Mr. Whalen?" Joe asked.

"Not a one," Whalen said. "But I trust the police to do a thorough job in finding out. And I don't think"—he leaned forward and looked meaningfully at Frank and Joe—"that we need any extra help in the matter. So I don't want to see you boys around the station anymore. Is that clear? Now, if you'll excuse me, I have to make some calls concerning the series we've been running on organized crime in the Bayport area. A couple of the sponsors want to pull out, and I've got to convince them that there will be big bucks in it if they stay with us." He picked up the phone, dialed a number, and turned around in his chair so that its tall leather back faced the Hardys.

"Come on," Marcy said, leading the Hardys out of the office.

"Nice guy," Joe commented, once they were in the hall.

"Yeah," Frank said. "Think we should stay on the case?" he asked Marcy. "Whalen doesn't seem to want us around."

"Don't worry about him," Marcy said, leading the Hardys down the flight of stairs. "Just report to me in the morning and tell me what you've found. Ted doesn't pay much attention to what actually goes on around the station. He'll never notice you're here. And if he does, I'll tell him you're going to do some spots on our 'Crimestoppers' show." The producer looked at her watch. "Now, I'm afraid I'm going to have to leave you on your own," she said. "I've got some work I need to finish before I can go home."

"Thanks, Marcy," Frank said. "We'll stop by your office in the morning."

"Well, what now?" Joe asked when Marcy had gone. "Should we start opening up closets looking for Clarence?"

"I've got a feeling the closets have already been checked," Frank said. "I've been thinking about that camera that almost fell on Steve and Debbie earlier."

"I still don't think it fell by accident," Joe said.

"I know you don't," Frank said. "But if someone

arranged for it to fall off the end of the boom, where was that person?"

"If I remember correctly," Joe said, "there's a whole network of catwalks under the ceiling of Studio A. Maybe somebody was up there when Steve and Debbie were squabbling over Matt's jacket—"

"—and they decided it was a perfect opportunity to get rid of some nosy kids," Frank finished. "So they removed a few screws from the camera and—boom!"

"So why don't we check out the catwalks?"

"I'm way ahead of you," Frank said, bounding up the stairs.

Back on the second floor, they headed in the opposite direction from Ted Whalen's office. When they came to the end of the hall, Frank pulled open the door marked Studio A Catwalks and looked inside.

There was a metal platform just beyond the door, bordered by a guardrail. A maze of narrow platforms extended out into the open space just below the ceiling and back into the shadows to the left.

Frank and Joe stepped quietly onto the platform. They could see Studio A below them to the right. The lights were on in the studio, but it was empty.

"Just like I remember it," Frank whispered, as they started down one of the catwalks.

Frank and Joe walked slowly, looking for signs of someone else having been there recently.

39

"Here," Joe said suddenly, pointing downward. "Footprints in the dust. They look fresh, too."

"That doesn't necessarily mean they were left by whoever dropped that camera," Frank pointed out.

"Let's see where they go," Joe suggested.

The trail of footprints led along the catwalk and around the corner to a second catwalk that ran directly above the studio. Halfway across, the footprints veered suddenly to one side of the catwalk. Joe gripped the railing and looked down. Bending over, he could see that directly below the catwalk was the top of a tall crane—the type TV crews called a boom—from which a camera had been suspended.

"This is the only boom up here," Joe reported. "So it has to be the one the camera was attached to. Whoever caused the camera to fall was standing right here."

"If only we could find somebody whose shoes fit those prints—"

Frank was cut off in midsentence by the sound of rushing footsteps from the far end of the catwalk.

A shadowy figure wearing a stocking over his face rushed toward Joe. The man lunged at Joe, pushed him over the railing, and then raced off. Joe gasped and tumbled over—falling headfirst toward the studio floor thirty feet below!

# 5 Home-Shopping Extravaganza

Joe grabbed desperately at the railing. He barely caught it in time to stop himself from hurtling into space.

Frank leaned over the guardrail and grasped Joe's wrist tightly. "I've got you! Let me pull you up."

"Don't get *me*," Joe said, hanging by one arm. "Get the guy who pushed me. He's getting away."

"No," Frank said. "You can't hang on that long. Pull yourself over the railing."

With Frank's help, Joe clambered over the rail and onto the catwalk. The Hardys looked for the attacker, but there was no sign of him. They hurried back into the hallway but found nobody there.

"I can't believe we let him get away," Joe said in a disgusted tone.

"Well, we're on to something, anyway," Frank said. "Whoever pushed you over that railing must be the same guy who unscrewed the camera."

"And ten-to-one it's the same person who nabbed Clarence," Joe added.

"If only we'd gotten a better look at him," Frank said with a sigh.

"Let's go back down to the studio," Joe suggested. "I think we've had enough fun up here for now."

Marcy Simons was in Studio A when the Hardys returned to the first floor. They quickly filled her in on what had happened.

"You've done all you can for now," she said. "The guards will make sure that Clarence isn't removed from the building without being seen—assuming that he's in here someplace, that is. Why don't you get a good night's sleep and come back here in the morning?"

"Fine with us," Joe said. "But I can't help thinking that Clarence is hidden around here waiting for someone to find him."

Frank nodded in agreement. "I hate to think we're letting him down."

"I know what you mean," Marcy said. "I'd really feel awful if something happened to him."

"But you're right, Marcy. It probably is time for us to go," Frank said.

42

The Hardys said good night to Marcy and headed out of the building to the parking lot.

As Joe drove their modified police van, Frank stared out the passenger window into the darkness. "So what do you think?" he said, turning to his brother. "Why would somebody want Clarence Kellerman out of the way?"

"I don't know," Joe replied. "But I get the impression that some of the people at the station don't like him."

"Like Matt Freeman," Frank said. "He seemed pretty happy that Clarence wasn't around. I wonder why."

"It's obvious," Joe said. "With Clarence gone, Matt will probably be the new host of 'The Four O'Clock Scholar.' I don't know much about the TV business, but I bet Matt would get a lot more money if he hosted two shows."

"True," Frank said. "And it was awfully suspicious that Matt just happened to be in the studio next door when Clarence turned up missing. It could be just a coincidence, though."

"And what about that Whalen guy?" Joe asked. "He sounded like he was anxious to get Clarence and his show off the air."

"But he doesn't have to kidnap him to do it," Frank replied. "He could just fire him and cancel the show."

"That makes sense," Joe said. "But I don't think we should write him off as a suspect. He could have

43

other reasons for kidnapping Clarence. I think we'd better talk to a few more people around the station tomorrow."

"Good idea," Frank said. "In the meantime, let's go see if some of the gang is still over at Mr. Pizza."

"Now you're talking," Joe said.

Five minutes later, the Hardys walked in the front door of their favorite pizza parlor to find that most of the Bayport High School students who had been at the show had already left for the evening. But Chet Morton was still hunched over a last slice of pizza, and Callie and Iola were sipping soft drinks.

"Hey, Frank," Callie said. "We thought you guys would never get here. Don't tell me you've gotten caught up in another investigation."

"How did you guess," Frank said with a grin as he slid into the chair next to his girlfriend. "I see Chet's into his second course already."

"Nah," Chet said. "I finished the second course a long time ago. This is dessert."

"So what's it about?" Iola wanted to know.

"What's what about?" Joe asked innocently.

"The case," Iola said impatiently. "What are you investigating? Is Clarence in any danger? Where is he?"

"Why should we tell you?" Joe teased. "You didn't save us any pizza."

"Anyway, it's top secret," Frank said. "We can't say anything about it yet."

"Come on, Frank," Callie said. "I bet you know

all sorts of juicy secrets about why Clarence wasn't there tonight, exactly the kind of things I'd love to tell all my friends about."

"And that's why we can't tell you," Joe said. "Because you'd tell all your friends."

"Okay, okay," Iola said with a laugh. "But you'd better tell us all about it when it's over. Or I'll never talk to you again."

Chet looked up from his pizza. "Gee, Iola," he said. "If you keep making promises like that, they may never tell you about the case."

The next morning, as the Hardys strode up to the front door of the WBPT studios, Joe saw Ted Whalen in the lobby of the station. The station manager was snapping orders at a nervous-looking receptionist, who was standing behind her desk.

"Uh-oh," Joe whispered. "I thought Marcy said this guy didn't pay attention to what's going on around the station."

"It looks like he's making an exception this morning," Frank said.

Whalen turned and saw the Hardys walk into the lobby. "You two!" he snapped. "I thought I told you to get out and stay out."

"Look, Mr. Whalen—" Joe began.

"I mean it!" Whalen boomed. "Victoria, show them to the door."

"I'm afraid you'll have to leave," said the young, blond receptionist, taking Joe by one arm and Frank by the other. She opened the door and gestured them through. As they walked past her, she whispered, "Marcy Simons wants to talk to you. Go in the back door where Terrible Ted here can't see you."

"What's gotten into him?" Joe whispered. "He wasn't like this when we met him yesterday."

"Do the names Steve and Debbie ring a bell?" Victoria replied.

Frank shook his head and sighed as Victoria closed the door behind them. "I knew it was a mistake to let that pair help search for Clarence."

"I wonder what they've done now," Joe said.

"I don't even want to think about it," Frank said. "Come on. Let's find the back door."

Frank and Joe walked through the parking lot that bordered one side of the building and into a door recessed into a shallow alcove toward the rear. A guard standing just inside the door nodded as the Hardys walked past. Marcy Simons's office was about fifty feet down the hall.

Marcy, seated behind her desk, looked up at the Hardys as they entered. "I'm glad to see you got in. I guess Ted didn't catch you."

"He did," Frank told her, "but we took an alternate route to your office."

"Victoria said that Steve and Debbie were responsible for his bad mood," Joe said. "What happened?"

"Those two loudmouth friends of yours cornered him in his office first thing this morning," Marcy explained. "They wanted to know where he was at the time of the crime. Needless to say, he had no interest in talking to them. When they wouldn't leave his office, he had a couple of guards throw them out."

"But what's that got to do with us?" Joe asked.

"He thinks Steve and Debbie are working with you," Marcy said. "He stormed into my office and announced that neither you nor your friends are to be allowed anywhere near the station."

"Do you want us to leave?" Frank asked.

"Of course not," Marcy said. "Just steer clear of Ted and make sure that those two overbearing brats keep as low a profile as possible."

"We'll do our best," Frank said.

Marcy leaned back in her chair. "I suppose you want to know what's new on the Clarence Kellerman front."

The Hardys nodded.

"Unfortunately, there's nothing much to report," Marcy said. "We've looked around the building, but there's no sign of him. If he's here, he's very well hidden. The guards are still posted at the doors."

"What about Clarence's family?" Joe asked. "Have you talked to them about him?"

"I'm afraid Clarence doesn't have much in the way of immediate family," Marcy said. "He was divorced nearly ten years ago. I talked to his ex-wife on the phone last night, and she hasn't heard from him in ages."

47

"What about children?" Frank asked. "Or parents?"

"None of the above," Marcy said. "He doesn't have any kids, and his parents died years ago. Believe me, we've already checked into that. He lives alone in a house not far from the station. The police went there yesterday and looked around, but they haven't turned up any clues."

Frank looked at Joe. "We don't have a whole lot of leads here, do we? Maybe we'd better talk to some more people around the station."

Joe nodded and said, "Thanks for filling us in, Marcy. We'll be around the station if you need us."

"Good luck," Marcy said. "Just don't let Ted Whalen catch you snooping around."

When they left Marcy's office, Frank looked at the rows of doorways that lined the hallway. "Well, let's get back on the trail. Who should we talk to first?"

"Good question," Joe said. "I— Hey, do you hear something in Studio A?"

Frank cocked an ear toward the studio door. "Yeah. Sounds like a show going on. Want to take a look?"

"Sure," Joe said. "Something exciting *always* happens to us when we go into Studio A."

"That's one way of looking at it," Frank said.

Joe pushed open the studio door, and the Hardys stepped inside. As they had guessed, there was a television show in progress. The first thing Frank and Joe saw was a pair of camera operators training their cameras on a plump man with a mustache who wore a pinstripe suit. The man was holding up a gold chain and delivering a line of rapid-fire patter to a microphone dangling from overhead. Frank noticed a sign to one side of the set that read WBPT Home-Shopping Extravaganza.

"This beautiful gold chain," the plump man said, "can be yours for the incredibly low, ridiculously low, unbelievably low price of just nineteen dollars and ninety-five cents, marked down from two hundred dollars because we believe in bringing you the greatest, the most fantastic, the most mind-boggling bargains we possibly can. We buy wholesale to keep the prices down, which means incredible savings for you. To purchase this beautiful twenty-four-karat gold-finish chain, just call the WBPT Home-Shopping Extravaganza hot line and have your credit card number ready. Our operators are standing by."

"Here's your chance," Frank said to his brother. "I know you've always wanted one of those."

"Sorry," Joe said. "I didn't bring my credit card with me. In fact, I don't even have a credit card."

"I'm sure he'll take cash," Frank said.

One of the camera operators, an older man with thinning hair and close-set eyes, turned and eyed Frank and Joe suspiciously. "You kids will have to leave," he said. "We're shooting a live TV show here."

"We'd just like to ask the host some questions when the show is over," Frank said. "It won't take long."

The cameraman studied the Hardys for a moment. "Say, aren't you the kids who caught the Masked Marauder? I remember you guys. Well, I guess it'll be okay if you stick around."

"Thanks," Joe said. "Who's the guy holding the chain?"

"That's Fred Dunlap," the cameraman replied. "He and his brother Al produce and write the home-shopping show by themselves. Whoops, it's time for me to do a close-up on the chain. Talk to you later."

When the show ended, Fred Dunlap mopped his forehead with a handkerchief and stepped down off the set. Joe looked toward the stage, where another heavy-set man was stepping out from behind a flat. He looked like a younger version of Fred Dunlap, except that his mustache was reddish in color while Fred's was brown.

"Al Dunlap?" Joe whispered to Frank, who nodded.

"Excuse me, Mr. Dunlap," Joe said, stepping into the brightly lit area around the stage. "Do you mind if we talk to you about Clarence Kellerman?"

"Which Mr. Dunlap do you want to talk to?" Al asked. "Me or Fred?"

Fred Dunlap laughed. "We're always happy to talk about"—he twisted his face into an expression almost identical to Clarence's familiar goofy smile —"your old buddy Clarence."

"Hey," Joe said. "That's a pretty good impression of Clarence. You sound just like him."

"I've worked around him for a long time," Fred said, chuckling. "Maybe too long."

"Actually, we'd like to talk to both of you," Frank said. "We were wondering when you last saw Mr. Kellerman."

Al Dunlap wrinkled his forehead as he thought about Frank's question. Frank decided that Al was the more serious of the two brothers. He hadn't even cracked a smile at Fred's imitation of Clarence. But Fred had a carefree and likable air about him.

"He was in the studio yesterday," Al said finally, "while we were doing our Sunday edition."

"Yesterday?" Joe asked, becoming excited. "You actually saw Clarence yesterday?"

"Sure," Fred said, nodding. "I remember seeing him around here for a while, then he said he was going off to the basement to look for props for his show. You know, for one of those crazy stunts he likes to pull."

"Do you remember what time that was?" Frank asked.

"Early afternoon," Al said. "Probably about one o'clock or so."

51

"Where's the basement?" Joe asked. "We'd like to take a look around."

"Just down the hall," Fred said, gesturing with his hand. "Behind the door marked Storage Area. It's where they keep old props and stuff."

"Thanks for your help," Frank said.

"Anytime, guys," Fred said heartily.

Frank and Joe left the studio and headed for the basement. "This is the hottest lead we've turned up yet," Frank said. "If Fred and Al Dunlap saw Clarence at one o'clock yesterday afternoon, that means he was still here four hours after the receptionist saw him arrive at nine."

"Right," Joe said. "Which means that the Dunlaps may have seen him right before he disappeared. And Clarence told them he was going to the basement. Maybe there'll be a clue down there."

"Maybe Clarence himself is in the basement," Frank added.

The door labeled Storage Area was unlocked. Frank pulled it open and started down the old stone steps inside. The air was musty and damp. The only light came through the door they had just opened.

Behind his brother, Joe said, "I hope there's a light switch down here somewhere."

"Me, too," Frank said. "Maybe we should go back up and get a flashlight."

Suddenly the door behind Joe slammed shut, and the staircase was plunged into total darkness.

Joe felt his way up the stairs. He grabbed the door and pulled. It wouldn't move.

"Open the door," Frank said urgently.

"Impossible," Joe replied grimly. "I can't get it open. We're locked in!"

# 6 Where There's Smoke

"What do you mean, we're locked in?" Frank asked, groping his way past Joe on the stairs and giving the doorknob a tug.

"I mean just what it sounds like I mean," Joe replied. "Read my lips."

"I can't read your lips," Frank said. "It's too dark." The door rattled uselessly as he pulled on the knob. "Yeah, it's locked all right."

"Thanks for checking," Joe muttered. "Nice to see you trust my judgment."

"What I want to know is, did someone lock us in here on purpose?" Frank asked.

"It wouldn't surprise me if someone did," Joe replied. "But right now, I think our first priority should be to try to get out of here."

The brothers began pounding on the door and shouting. When nobody had come to let them out after five minutes, Frank said, "Forget it, Joe. Either the door's too thick or no one's around. Nobody can hear us."

"That's just great," Joe said. "We should be down there looking for Clarence, not groping around in the dark."

"I think we'd better start looking for a light switch," Frank said. "If we could see better, we might be able to figure out how to get out of here."

One side of the staircase on which the Hardys were standing was bordered by a stone wall, the other by a railing. Frank ran his hands along the wall but found only solid stone. The stone felt damp and slightly dirty, like the wall of a cave.

"No luck," Frank said. "I can't find a switch."

"I'll look down here," Joe said, making his way carefully down the stairs. At the bottom, he extended his arms in front of himself, feeling his way in the darkness.

"Be careful," Frank said, following his brother down the stairs. "We don't know what's down here."

"Al and Fred said that there are a lot of old props stored here," Joe said. "If we can't find a light switch, maybe we can find something else we can use."

"Like the key to that door?" Frank asked.

"I'll settle for that," Joe said.

Frank groped around tentatively. "Ouch," he said. "I banged into some kind of wire cage."

"A cage?" Joe asked. "Are they keeping animals down here?"

"I doubt it," Frank said. "That would be pretty cruel."

"Here's some stuff," Joe said. "Could be props for a TV show. There are some books and an old candleholder and— Hey, this feels like something useful."

"What is it?" Frank asked. "A telephone to call out of here?"

"No," Joe replied. "I think it's an oil lamp. Smells like it has oil in it, too. And—ah! Here's a book of matches."

"Now if you can just find a refrigerator and some food," Frank said, "we don't have to worry about getting out. We can just live down here for a few years."

Joe struck one of the matches. The glow dimly illuminated his face and Frank's. He lifted the glass cover of the lamp and held the flame to the wick. After about ten seconds, the wick caught the flame and began to glow brightly enough so that Frank and Joe could see some details of the room around them.

The first thing they saw was the cage that Frank had bumped into. The cage was made of wire mesh that was set in a tall metal frame, and it blocked off a portion of the basement. There was a door set in the frame with a large padlock on it. Joe held the lamp up to the cage, but the light wasn't strong enough to allow them to see what was inside.

Frank and Joe looked around the rest of the basement. The room seemed huge, and most of it was hidden in shadow, too far away to be illuminated by the weak glow of the lamp. All across the visible part of the room, the Hardys could see piles of old boxes and a variety of objects stacked from floor to ceiling. They could make out a collection of chairs and sofas, paintings and table lamps, television monitors and bookcases. A huge blue plush elephant stared out from between two plastic palm trees. A pink plastic flamingo hung upside down in the middle of a child's jungle gym.

"Wow," Joe said. "Maybe you weren't kidding when you said we could move in here. You name it, it looks like they've got it in this place."

"Let's just concentrate on getting out of here," Frank said. "This isn't my idea of a comfortable living space."

The brothers began to move cautiously around the room. Suddenly, Joe stopped in his tracks.

"Did you just make a funny noise?" he asked his brother.

"No," Frank said. "I thought you did."

"It sounded like someone whimpering," Joe said quietly. "Listen. There it is again."

The brothers listened carefully. The sound seemed to be coming from somewhere among the vast piles of props.

The brothers stared at each other.

"Clarence!" they both cried at the same time.

Frank began rummaging through a pile of boxes. "Come on," he said. "We've got to track down the source of that noise. Clarence must be in here somewhere."

"It came from over here," Joe said, pointing into the center of a pile of junk.

"No," Frank said. "I think it was over here." He pointed to a pile of half-crushed boxes stacked in a corner of the room.

The whimpering began again, louder this time.

"We're both wrong," Joe said. "It came from right here." He hurried over to a long black trunk lying on the floor. A thick gray padlock attached to one side of the lid held the trunk securely closed.

"There's somebody in the trunk," Frank said, kneeling down. "But it's locked."

"We'll break the lock," Joe said, picking up a large hammer from a shelf full of tools and handing the lamp to Frank. "It looks pretty old. I bet I can shatter it with this hammer. Get out of the way."

Joe swung the hammer at the lock and hit it so hard that the trunk shuddered. The muffled sound from inside became even louder, but the lock remained stubbornly in place.

"Hold on, Clarence!" Joe shouted urgently. "We'll get you out of there as fast as we can."

Joe swung the hammer again, striking the lock even harder than before. The lock shook wildly, but did not break. The voice inside the trunk yelled something unintelligible.

"Old Clarence is going to have quite a headache when this is over," Frank said.

"I'm sure he'd rather have a headache than be stuck inside that trunk," Joe replied.

He smashed the hammer against the lock one more time. With a crumpling sound, the core dropped out of the lock and it sprung open with a snap. Joe dropped the hammer and removed the remains of the lock from the trunk.

"Help me open it," he said, wrestling the trunk away from the surrounding boxes so that he could get a good grip on the lid. Frank set the lamp down on a box and moved to the other end of the trunk.

With a sharp yank from Frank and Joe, the lid popped open. Inside was a familiar black-haired figure tied up in thick rope with a rolled-up handkerchief in her mouth.

Joe and Frank looked down at the figure in astonishment.

"Debbie!" Joe shouted. "What are you doing in there?"

"Mmmphh!" declared Debbie through the handkerchief.

"Right," Frank said, kneeling down beside the trunk. "Let's get her untied."

"Maybe we can leave the gag in her mouth," Joe suggested.

Frank gave Joe a sharp look.

"Okay, okay, I was only kidding," Joe said, helping to remove the ropes that bound Debbie's arms. Frank pulled the rolled-up handkerchief out of her mouth.

"What were you trying to do?" Debbie shrieked angrily. "Kill me? I feel like I've been rolling around inside a cement mixer."

"I had to break the lock on the trunk," Joe said defensively. "You did want to get out, didn't you?"

Debbie combed her hair back with her fingers, then pulled herself out of the trunk with the Hardys' help. "Well, I guess so," she said, as she brushed the dust off her jacket and jeans. "But you could have at least given me a warning."

"What happened?" Frank asked. "How did you end up in there?"

"Steve and I were looking around the basement, trying to find Clarence, when the lights suddenly went out," Debbie explained. "We looked for the light switch, but we couldn't find it."

"How long ago was that?" Frank asked.

"I'm not sure," Debbie said, glancing at her watch. "I guess about twenty minutes ago."

"What happened then?" Joe asked.

"Somebody must have hit me over the head," Debbie said, "because the next thing I remember was finding myself tied up inside that trunk. I tried to call out, but I couldn't because I had the gag in my mouth. Then you started pounding really hard right next to my head."

"Where's Steve?" Frank asked.

"How would I know?" Debbie said with a shrug. "And why should I care? Maybe he's the one who hit me over the head."

"Oh, great," Joe said. "Now we've got two missing persons, Steve and Clarence."

A muffled voice suddenly came from another trunk.

"Well, I think we just found one of them," Frank said.

"I vote for Clarence," Joe said, picking up the hammer. "Here we go again."

Joe whacked the lock on the side of the trunk until it popped apart. Then he and Frank pried the lid open.

Steve was inside, tied up and gagged just as Debbie had been. Joe untied the ropes while Frank removed the gag from Steve's mouth.

"Where've you guys been?" Steve said as soon as he caught his breath. "If you're such great detectives, why didn't you get me out of that trunk sooner?"

"We're detectives, not magicians," Frank said.

"We can always tie you up again and find out how long it takes next time," Joe suggested.

"Could take a month," Frank said. "Assuming we get around to it at all."

"That's too soon for me," Debbie said, glaring down at Steve. "Some help you were when the lights went out. You couldn't even find the way back upstairs."

"That's because I was following *you*," Steve said. "You couldn't find your way out of a phone booth if you tried."

"Knock it off, you two," Joe said. "We still have to find our way out of this place, you know."

"What?" Steve exclaimed. "I thought you were here to rescue us."

"We've, ah, managed to get ourselves locked in," Frank said.

"Oh, that's terrific," Steve said. "Now we're all trapped down here."

"Don't worry," Joe said with more confidence than he felt. "We'll think of some way out."

"By the way," Frank said, "we heard that you two had a little conversation with Ted Whalen this morning. Would you mind telling us what happened?"

"I thought it would be a good idea to talk to the manager of the station about Clarence's disappearance," Steve said.

"Exactly what did you say to Whalen?" Joe asked. "He was pretty angry by the time we got here."

"We hardly got a chance to say anything at all," Debbie replied. "He chased us out of his office almost immediately."

"Obviously he was trying to cover something up," Steve said. "And we told him that, too. Why else wouldn't he talk to us?"

"Maybe he's got better things to do," Joe suggested. "And maybe you were being kind of pushy."

"Well, maybe Debbie did come on a bit strong," Steve said, "but I'm convinced that Whalen is involved with Clarence's disappearance somehow. The only problem is how to prove it."

"I think we should follow Ted Whalen until he leads us to Clarence," Debbie suggested.

"I think you two had better stay about five miles away from Ted Whalen," Frank said. "If he so much as sees you in the station, he's going to throw us all out for good."

"That's not our problem," Steve said. "Our problem is finding Clarence. And getting—"

"Do you smell smoke?" Debbie asked, looking alarmed.

"Sure I smell smoke," Steve said. "It's coming from the oil lamp."

"No, it doesn't smell like that kind of smoke," Debbie said. "It smells completely different."

"I think maybe you should put your nose in the shop for repairs," Steve said. "I don't smell any smoke at all."

"I do," Frank said.

"Yeah," Joe said. "So do I."

Frank picked up the oil lamp and held it over his head. "Look around. Can you see any smoke?"

"Yes!" Joe declared. "Over there."

He pointed at a vent placed high in the wall over

a stack of boxes. A thick cloud of black smoke poured out of the vent.

"Now we've got an even bigger problem than finding Clarence," Frank said.

"Right," Joe said. "If that smoke keeps pouring out of there like that, none of us is going to be able to breathe!"

# 7 Hot on the Trail

"Where's it coming from?" Debbie cried, looking at the thick black cloud near the vent.

"It looks like somebody's pumping it directly into the ventilation system, maybe from right outside the basement," Frank said. "Somebody apparently wants to make sure we stop our investigation."

"Everybody get down on the floor," Joe said. "Smoke rises to the ceiling, so we'll be able to breathe longer near the ground."

"We've got to think fast," Frank said as he dropped to the floor with the others. "How can we get out of this basement?"

"Oh," Debbie said. "Actually, that's no problem." She held up a small key with a tag on it marked Basement. "I took this from the reception-ist's desk while she wasn't looking. I thought it might come in handy down here."

"Why didn't you show us that key before?" Frank asked, exasperated.

"I just forgot I had it," Debbie said.

"Forgot?" Joe said, as he took the key from Debbie. "We were all trapped down here. How could you forget that you had the key?"

"I was tied up unconscious in a trunk for twenty minutes," Debbie retorted. "I don't do my best thinking under those conditions."

"Okay, okay. I apologize," Joe said.

"Let's get moving," Frank said. "Cover your faces so you don't breathe any smoke. You two can use those handkerchiefs you were gagged with."

Steve and Debbie buried their faces in the hand-kerchiefs while Frank and Joe pulled their shirts up over their noses. With Joe leading the way and Frank holding the lamp, the four teenagers hurried across the basement and up the stairs.

Joe plunged the key into the lock and rattled the doorknob. The door popped open.

"Thank goodness!" Debbie cried as she stumbled into the hallway. "That smoke made my eyes sting."

"It would have done more damage than that if we'd been down there any longer," Joe said, pock-eting the key.

"Look at this," Frank said, pointing at a closet door to his right. It was closed, but wisps of smoke were coming out from underneath it. He pulled the door open. Inside the closet was a metal trash can. The can was covered tightly, and a wide rubber tube ran from a hole in the lid to an air vent set low in the closet wall.

Joe touched the side of the lid and immediately jerked back his hand. "It's hot! There's got to be a fire in there."

Frank looked desperately up and down the hallway. Finally he spotted an emergency fire case about ten feet away. He broke the glass and pulled out the ax inside. A fire alarm began to ring.

"Somebody get the extinguisher!" he cried, rushing to the trash can and knocking the lid off with a clean swipe of the ax. Thick greasy smoke and bright tongues of flame leaped out of the can.

With the fire extinguisher in hand, Joe ran to the trash can and sprayed it until the flames began to sputter. After a few minutes the fire was out, but the hallway was filled with smoke.

A pair of guards had rushed down the hall in response to the fire alarm. The Hardys explained what had happened, and the guards inspected the trash can.

"Well, that's obviously where the smoke in the basement came from," Frank said. "Now if we only knew who started it."

Steve began to cough. "I need fresh air," he gasped. He rushed to the end of the hallway and pushed open the door that led out to the parking lot. Then he stepped back inside and motioned to the others.

"Come here," he said. "Quick."

Debbie hurried to the door and peered outside. "What is it?"

Steve pointed at a black limousine and said, "There's Ted Whalen."

Joe joined the pair and looked out the door, craning to see over the top of Steve's red head. Ted Whalen stood next to the large car. Two heavyset men in dark suits stood beside him. One was short and muscular, the other was tall and broad-shouldered.

"I don't like the looks of those guys," Debbie said in a low voice. "I bet they were the ones who grabbed Clarence. Let's go ask them a few questions."

Joe grabbed Debbie's arm as she started out the door. "If Ted Whalen sees you out there, he'll call the police."

"No way," Steve said. "Criminals don't call the police. They're afraid of the police."

"From the looks of those big guys he's got with him, he may not *need* to call the police," Frank observed.

"He could have one of those gorillas sit on you until you're too old to be a problem," Joe said to Steve.

"And I'd like to point out that being in the company of people who look like thugs isn't necessarily evidence of a crime," Frank said. "Maybe they're relatives or friends."

"Want to bet?" Steve challenged, and then pointed out the door. "Look at that."

As Ted Whalen slid into the passenger seat of the black car, the short, stocky man reached into the inner pocket of his jacket and pulled out a gun. He checked to see if it was loaded, then put it back in his coat pocket and slid into the rear seat next to the tall man. The chauffeur, who had been sitting in the car all along, revved the engine and began to drive away.

"A gun!" Debbie cried. "You can't say that doesn't look suspicious."

"They're getting away!" Steve shouted. "We've got to follow them."

"Come on," Debbie said. "We'll use my car."

"No," Steve said. "We'll use my car."

"We'll use our van," Frank said. "I don't like the idea of you guys following Ted Whalen through the streets of Bayport on your own."

The Hardys, Steve, and Debbie slipped into the parking lot as Ted Whalen's limousine turned onto the street. As Frank opened the door of the Hardy van and climbed into the driver's seat, the other three simultaneously went to open the passenger door.

"Hey," Frank said, settling down behind the steering wheel. "There isn't room up front for four people."

69

"I'll share the seat with Joe," Debbie said, as she climbed into the van and perched herself on the inside edge of the seat. "There's room for both of us."

"Look, Debbie," Joe said with a sigh, "you can have the whole seat, okay? I'll ride in the back with Steve."

When his three passengers were settled, Frank pulled out of the parking lot and bolted in the direction Ted Whalen's limousine had vanished. As Frank steered the van, he spotted the limo at the next traffic light. A moment later the light turned green, and Whalen's chauffeur stepped on the gas. Frank did the same.

"Maybe he'll lead us to Clarence," Debbie said. "I'll bet that's where they're heading now."

"Nah," Steve said. "Clarence is probably back at the TV station. Whalen will lead us to the rest of the gang that kidnapped Clarence."

Joe stared at Steve. "Gang? What gang?"

"You don't think Ted Whalen is in this alone, do you?" Steve asked.

"I don't know if Ted Whalen is in this at all," Joe retorted. "So far, nothing that he's done proves he's behind Clarence's disappearance."

"If Whalen doesn't have a gang," Steve said, "who trapped us in the basement and tried to kill us?"

"We don't know if Whalen is behind it in the first place," Joe reminded him.

70

Steve continued as if he hadn't heard Joe. "Guys like Whalen don't like to get their hands dirty. That's what he's got those thugs for. I bet they're the ones who bopped me and Debbie over the head."

Whalen's car veered onto a side street. As the limo turned at an angle to the Hardy's van, Frank saw the tall man in the backseat roll down his window and look out at them.

"Oh, no," Frank said, following the limousine onto the tree-lined street. "They've spotted us."

"And they've got guns!" Debbie cried. "They'll probably start shooting at us."

"In broad daylight, in the middle of a residential neighborhood?" Joe asked. "From a clearly marked car belonging to a prominent local businessman? Get real!"

"These are desperate characters," Steve said seriously. "You never know what they'll do."

"True," Frank joked. "After that scene with Whalen this morning, he's probably given his men orders to shoot you and Debbie on sight."

Suddenly the limousine accelerated and pulled rapidly away from the Hardy van.

"Speed up," Steve said. "You can't let them get away."

"Haven't you ever heard of speed limits?" Frank asked. "It's dangerous, not to mention illegal, to drive fast through a neighborhood like this. People live around here."

71

"Nobody told that to Whalen's driver," Steve pointed out. "He just floored the accelerator."

"They're getting away!" Debbie cried.

Far ahead, the limousine turned onto a side street and vanished from sight.

"They're gone," Steve said. "What do we do now?"

"Keep looking for them," Frank said. "They can't be too far."

"Turn that way," Joe said, pointing in the direction the limousine had gone. "Maybe we can still pick up the trail."

Frank steered around the corner, but there was no sign of Whalen's car. He made a few more turns without sighting the limousine.

"I've got an idea," Joe said suddenly. "Marcy told us that Whalen came from an old, rich family. Ten to one he lives in Bayside Estates, where all the most expensive houses are."

"Right," Frank said. "And Bayside Estates is up here." He turned the van down a street lined with trees and huge lawns.

"There sure are some awfully big houses around here," Debbie said as they passed several mansions.

"There," Joe said, pointing toward the driveway of a mansion on the left. "Isn't that the limo Ted Whalen was in?"

A black limousine like the one Frank had been following was parked in the driveway. The drive curved in front of a large house that had white columns in front of its redbrick facade.

"You're right, Joe," Frank said. "Look at that mailbox. It's got the name Whalen on it."

Frank drove past the house, parked the van about a hundred feet down the road, and turned the motor off.

"Well, what do we do now?" Joe asked. "We've found out where Ted Whalen lives, but I don't see any guys in black suits with guns hanging around the yard."

"I think we ought to get a closer look," Debbie said.

"That might not be such a hot idea," Frank said.

"It's a great idea," Steve said, climbing out the back door. Debbie quickly climbed out of the passenger door.

"Maybe we should just drive off and let those two get into trouble all by themselves," Joe suggested.

"Bad idea," Frank said, opening his door and climbing out of the van. "If they get in trouble, we get in trouble, too. Remember, Whalen thinks they're working with us."

"Let's just hope Whalen and his pals don't see us," Joe said. He climbed to the front of the van and jumped out the passenger door. "Let's go."

Steve and Debbie were already halfway across the lawn and running toward the mansion as Frank and Joe started after them. For a moment the Hardys could hear the two would-be detectives squabbling over which side of the house to look at first. Then they saw the twosome disappear into a small grove of trees next to the house. By the time

73

Frank and Joe reached the grove, Steve was halfway up a tree, trying to get a look through one of the first-floor windows.

"What are you doing?" Frank asked, looking up at Steve as the red-haired teen climbed out on a limb.

"Checking out the house," Steve said. "Maybe I'll see something that'll give us a clue."

"Maybe you'll get us all arrested as prowlers," Joe said.

"I think we should sneak into the basement," Debbie said. "There's a door just down there." She pointed at the wall of the house.

"If you get caught, you could be charged with breaking and entering," Frank said.

"We're just trying to save poor Clarence Kellerman," Debbie insisted. "That's no crime."

"Hey," Steve whispered, clinging tightly to the far end of the limb. "I can see somebody inside. It looks like Ted Whalen—"

"It is Ted Whalen," said a new voice. The Hardys and Debbie turned to see the short muscular man who'd been in Whalen's car standing next to the corner of the house. He had thick black hair slicked straight back from his forehead and wore a dark suit and tie. He glared at the four teenagers.

"And you kids are trespassing on Mr. Whalen's property," he continued. "I'm afraid this is the end of the line for you."

He reached into his coat pocket, pulled out a gun, and pointed it directly at Joe.

# 8 Narrow Escape

Joe stared at the gun-wielding man in surprise. "We can explain what we're doing here." He glanced desperately at his brother. "Isn't that right, Frank?"

"Right," Frank said. "We were, um, looking for Mr. Whalen. We wanted to talk to him for a minute."

"Well, Mr. Whalen doesn't want to talk to you," the man said in a menacing tone. "And he doesn't much like people hanging around his house and looking in his windows, either. You'd better come up with a better explanation of what you're doing here or you're going to be in big, big trouble."

"We're trying to find out what happened to

Clarence Kellerman," Steve said, still sitting on the limb of the tree.

"Yeah," Debbie said. "And we think Mr. Whalen had something to do with it. He'd better have some good answers himself or *he's* going to be the one who's in trouble."

There was a noise from the corner of the house. The Hardys turned to see Ted Whalen walking around the corner. The tall, broad-shouldered man was with him. Whalen's jaw fell when he saw the four teenagers clustered around the tree.

"Not you kids again!" he said angrily. "Don't you ever give up? I told you that I never wanted to see the four of you again—and I meant it."

Steve leaped out of the tree and, with a thump, landed on the ground. "What are you covering up, Whalen?" he said. "Where do you have Clarence Kellerman stashed away?"

"What in the world are you talking about?" Whalen snapped.

Frank took a deep breath. "What Steve is trying to say is that we'd like to question you about Clarence Kellerman's disappearance."

"One thing we'd like to know, Mr. Whalen—" Joe began.

"I'll handle the questions, Hardy," Steve interrupted. "What did you do to Clarence, Whalen? Did you want him out of the way because he didn't fit your plans for the station?"

"You're way out of line," Whalen said hotly, pointing a finger at Steve. "I had nothing whatsoever to do with Clarence Kellerman's disappearance. And if I wanted him out of the way, I'd simply give him a pink slip. I run the station—or have you forgotten that?"

"Then why do you keep guys with guns around you?" Debbie asked. "Do you need mobsters to help you run the station?"

"These men happen to be my personal bodyguards," Whalen replied. "I've kept them by my side whenever I've left the station for the past three weeks."

"And why does a station manager need bodyguards?" Steve asked. "To do his dirty work for him?"

"WBPT news has been running a hard-hitting series of stories on organized crime in the Bayport area," Whalen said. "My life has been threatened several times. I won't be intimidated by those who'd like to stand in the way of the truth, but I'd be foolish to risk my life. So I keep a guard around me. Not that it's any of your business."

Joe looked at his brother. "Actually, that's a pretty reasonable answer," he said. "We heard you talking about that crime series back at the station."

Frank nodded. "Maybe we've been mistaken. Sorry we bothered you, Mr. Whalen."

"Hey, I've got lots more questions," Debbie protested.

"Yeah, so do I," Steve said.

"Write them down and send them to Mr. Whalen in a letter," Frank said, grabbing Steve by the arm and pulling him toward the van. "We've got better things to do than hang around here."

"I don't want you kids coming near my house anymore, do you hear me?" Whalen called after them. "And I don't want you around WBPT either. I'll call the police if I see you again. Don't forget that."

"We won't," Joe said.

Half walking, half running, the four teenagers rushed back to the van and climbed inside.

"I don't believe this," Frank said once they were safely in the van. "You two clowns almost got us shot back there just because you have some sort of crazy idea that Ted Whalen is guilty."

"Well, I still think he's guilty," Debbie said. "And I really did have lots more questions to ask."

"I thought you Hardys were supposed to be really brave," Steve said. "I figured facing a gun would be nothing to guys like you."

"We'll face down guns if there's a reason to," Joe snapped. "But we have no real reason to suspect Whalen."

Frank revved up the van and started driving away from Whalen's mansion. "Where's your evidence that proves Whalen had something to do with Clarence's disappearance?" he asked.

"Whalen's conceited and I don't like him," said Steve. "Isn't that enough?"

"No," Joe said. "If being conceited were a crime, then the jails would have been full a long time ago."

"Okay, everybody," Frank said. "Let's call a truce. At least until we get back to the TV station."

The foursome remained quiet during the drive back to WBPT. Frank swung into the lot and parked the van in a distant corner, where he hoped that Ted Whalen wouldn't notice it. As soon as they were out of the van, Debbie and Steve headed toward the building.

"You two stay out of trouble," Frank warned. "We don't want to have to bail you out again if Ted Whalen goes after you."

Back inside the WBPT building, the Hardys found Marcy Simons pacing angrily around her office, muttering something about Matt Freeman.

"More problems?" Joe asked. "I hope Matt Freeman hasn't disappeared, too."

"No," Marcy said, settling down behind her desk. "Just business problems this time. Matt's asking for double his normal salary to do both 'Faces and Places' and 'The Four O'Clock Scholar.' I suppose he deserves it; doing two shows is a lot of work. But I hate the idea of bringing it up to Ted Whalen."

"I gather Ted likes making money a lot more than passing it out," Frank said.

"You bet," Marcy replied. "Ted sees Clarence's disappearance as an ideal opportunity to cut costs. By having Matt do both jobs, Ted gets two hosts for the price of one."

"Except Matt doesn't see it that way," Joe said.

"Right," Marcy said.

"Do you think he'll get the raise?" Frank asked.

"Probably," Marcy replied, "but there'll be a lot of flak. Good talent is hard to find, and it would cost us a bundle just to locate a replacement for Clarence. So even at twice the salary, Matt's still a bargain. Don't tell him I said that, though."

"We won't," Joe assured her.

"Worst of all, the end result of all of this will probably be that Ted will cancel 'The Four O'Clock Scholar.' Anyway, that's really not your problem," Marcy said. "How's the search for Clarence coming along?"

"Not too well," Frank said. "We've got some questions for you, though. Are those big guys that Whalen keeps around him really bodyguards?"

Marcy laughed. "They do look frightening, don't they? Yes, Ted hired them a few weeks ago. There've been lots of nasty phone calls since we started airing that series on organized crime, and Ted got nervous. I don't think anything's going to come of it, though. Neither do the police. Anyway, the series is ending next week."

"Speaking of the police," Joe said, "how are they doing in the search for Clarence?"

"Not too well," Marcy said with a sigh. "They've questioned all of Clarence's neighbors as well as everyone at the station, but no leads so far."

Frank nodded. "We've been coming up empty, too."

"Do you want us to stay on the case?" Joe asked.

"Of course," Marcy said. "The police seem to be losing interest already. Apparently they've had other missing person cases like this and most of the investigations end up going nowhere, or the people return on their own. I told the police Clarence wasn't the type of person to walk out on his job and his coworkers like that," Marcy added. "He may have a strange sense of humor, but he also has a real sense of responsibility."

"That's not what Matt Freeman said yesterday," Frank said.

"Matt has his own reasons for not liking Clarence," Marcy said. "The two never got along very well, and Matt never made any secret of the fact that he'd like to have Clarence's job. Now he's got it."

Just then, the phone rang. The brothers turned to leave.

"Thanks, guys," Marcy said as she picked up the receiver. "Keep me posted on how things are going."

"We will," Frank promised. After the brothers left Marcy's office, they walked down the hallway. As they passed the engineering room next to Studio A, they spotted Matt Freeman having a conversation with two of the engineers.

"There's Matt," Frank said. "Why don't we talk to him now?"

"Good idea," Joe said. "He's the only person we

81

know so far with a clear-cut motive for getting rid of Clarence."

"Right," Frank said. "With Clarence out of the way, Matt stands to turn a pretty nice profit, from what Marcy tells us. Let's ask him a few questions."

The engineering room was lined with television monitors and banks of electronic equipment. A young engineer with curly brown hair sat before a console filled with dials and switches. As Frank watched, she pushed buttons and threw switches in response to commands that she was apparently receiving over a pair of headphones. Matt Freeman, who was talking to a second engineer, turned and smiled at the Hardys as they walked into the room.

"How are you doing, guys?" Freeman asked. "I hear you're looking for Clarence. Any luck?"

"Not much, Matt," Joe said. "I don't suppose you've heard anything about him yourself?"

"Not a thing," Freeman responded. "Like I said, maybe he'll come jumping out from behind the curtain Tuesday night and announce that all's well. If he does, I'm going to pop him one in the nose."

"Why?" Frank asked curiously.

"Why?" Freeman echoed. "Because it's a pretty stupid publicity stunt for him to pull, that's why."

"And because he'll probably want his job back?" Joe suggested.

Freeman's expression changed. "Very funny. You're not thinking that I might be glad that Clarence has disappeared, are you? And I hope you're not suggesting that I might have had something to do with his disappearance."

Frank flashed Joe a disapproving look. "We're not suggesting anything, Mr. Freeman."

"Good," Freeman said, turning back to the engineer. "Now go play detective someplace else. I'm busy right now."

"We were just on our way out," Frank said, tugging his brother's arm. "Come on, Joe."

Out in the hallway, Frank turned to Joe and said, "That was a dumb question. You really didn't expect him to answer it, did you?"

"Sorry," Joe said. "It just slipped out. Maybe I've been hanging around Steve and Debbie too long."

"Yeah," Frank agreed. "That pair is starting to take the edge off my detective technique, too."

Joe glanced at his watch. "Maybe we should call it a day and go home to get some dinner. I'm convinced we'll be back to our normal sharp-witted selves in the morning."

"I hate to quit at all," Frank said. "Clarence is still out there someplace, depending on somebody to find him. And it looks like we're the ones who will have to do it, not the police."

"Well, he'll probably still be there tomorrow," Joe said. "Let's go."

Frank and Joe walked back into the parking lot and climbed into the van. Joe decided to take the driver's seat this time. Frank unlocked the passenger side and climbed into the seat.

Joe frowned as he pulled open the door. "Didn't you lock the driver's side of the van when we got out earlier?" he asked.

"I'm almost positive I did," Frank said. "Why? Was it unlocked?"

"Yeah," Joe said. "But maybe you forgot to lock it when you got out, after all the confusion."

"Could be," Frank said. "Don't worry about it."

"Maybe we'd better have a talk with Steve and Debbie tomorrow," Joe said, as he drove down Bayport's main street. "If we let them run freely around the TV station looking for clues, they may cause more problems than they solve."

"You're right," Frank said, leaning back and stretching his legs. "They're smart enough to be on the quiz show, but sometimes they do some dumb things. Maybe we should try to call them tonight. What do you think?"

Frank turned and looked out the window of the van. He was beginning to relax a little now that they were away from the station. He hoped their investigation would go better after a night's sleep.

It was several seconds before he noticed that Joe hadn't answered his last question.

He turned to see his brother, perched at the wheel of the van, staring glassy-eyed out the front window. Then he noticed an acrid smell in the air, like ammonia or rubbing alcohol.

"Joe?" Frank asked. "Are you okay?"

Suddenly Joe slumped forward onto the steering

wheel. Like a heavy stone, his foot plunged down on the accelerator, and the van shot forward. Then it swerved to the right.

Frank looked through the windshield and realized that they were heading straight toward the front window of a store.

# 9 Deadly Fumes

Frank shoved his unconscious brother aside, grabbed the steering wheel, and desperately turned it to the left. The van skidded back onto the road. Frank heaved a sigh of relief.

But they weren't out of danger yet. As it veered away from the sidewalk, the van swung in front of a delivery truck that was barreling down the road. Frank grabbed the wheel and turned it just in time to avoid the truck. He swung back onto the road — right into the path of a car that was pulling out of a parking space. With another quick turn of the wheel, he avoided the car, too.

Other drivers had begun to honk loudly as the van zigzagged back and forth down the street.

Frank jostled his brother urgently, trying to bring him back to consciousness.

"Joe!" Frank shouted loudly. "What's the matter with you?"

His brother didn't respond. Instead, he slumped down into the seat. As he did, his foot slipped off the accelerator. Frank pushed him against the door of the van, then he squeezed halfway into the driver's seat, and stomped on the brake with his foot.

The van screeched to a halt in the center of the road. Trembling, Frank put the van into park, turned on the flashers, and then fell back into his seat. Suddenly he realized that his head was spinning—and not just from the effort of trying to control the van. He felt as though he had inhaled some kind of poison gas.

Frank leaped out of the passenger door and gulped down breaths of fresh air. Then he ran around the van and yanked open his brother's door. The younger Hardy tumbled out of the van into his arms.

"Hey, are you kids out of your minds?" a man shouted angrily.

Frank turned to see a nearby driver jump out of his car and run toward the Hardys. He was about to yell something else when he saw Joe slumped unconscious in Frank's arms.

"Something's wrong with my brother," Frank explained. "He collapsed while he was driving."

Frank dragged Joe's limp form to the curb in front of the van, out of the way of traffic. After a few seconds, Joe began to stir groggily.

"Want me to call an ambulance?" the driver asked. "Sorry I yelled at you. I thought you were one of those reckless drivers."

"Not usually," Frank said. "I think my brother's starting to wake up. Thanks for the offer, though."

After the man had left, Frank leaned into the cab of the van and looked around the driver's seat. He smelled the same acrid odor he had smelled earlier. He looked under the seat and saw the corner of a metal canister.

Frank reached under the seat and pulled out the canister. Holding it at arm's length, he placed it on the pavement some distance from where Joe was lying. The canister was open, and there was a foul-smelling liquid inside. The label on the outside of the canister was covered with chemical names that Frank didn't recognize.

He remembered how Joe had noticed earlier that the door of the van was unlocked. Someone must have jimmied the lock and placed the canister under the seat.

"W-What happened?" Joe asked groggily, pulling himself up on one elbow.

"You got a noseful of whatever's in that jar," Frank said, pointing at the canister. "I've got a feeling it's not something that human beings are supposed to breathe."

"Why am I lying on the side of the road?" Joe asked, looking around.

"Gravity, mostly," Frank said. "You passed out while you were driving."

Joe's eyes opened wide. "Passed out? While I was driving? I could have been killed!"

"I think that was the idea," Frank said quietly.

"How did it happen?" Joe asked as he slowly got to his feet. "Where did that jar come from?"

"I'm not sure," Frank answered. "But I think we'll be asking a few people back at WBPT about that tomorrow morning. Right now, we need to air out the van."

The Hardys pushed the van to the side of the road and opened all the doors. Frank found a plastic bag in the back of the van and fastened it around the mouth of the canister with a rubber band to keep the gas from escaping again. Then he and his brother headed straight for home.

The next morning, Frank and Joe entered the WBPT studios by the back door and walked down the hall to Marcy Simons's office.

"Do you know what this is?" Frank asked Marcy, placing the canister on her desk.

Marcy recoiled at the sight of the canister. "Get that stuff away from me!" she exclaimed. "That's poisonous. Breathe too much of it and you'll be out like a light."

"We know," Joe said. "We found out the hard way."

"The engineers use that stuff for really tough electronic cleaning jobs," Marcy said, "but only under carefully controlled conditions. They keep it under lock and key in a storage room. Where'd you get hold of it?"

"Somebody stuck it under the driver's seat in our van," Frank said, "knowing that one of us would breathe the stuff. Joe was the lucky one who got to try it out—and almost got both of us killed when he passed out at the wheel."

"That's terrible," Marcy said in a concerned voice. "Why would somebody do that?"

"Because the kidnapper doesn't want us getting any closer to Clarence," Joe said. "Yesterday's fire was set up to release smoke into the basement. Someone locked us down there and then tried to kill us, Steve, and Debbie."

"The funny thing is," Frank said, "we're not even close to finding Clarence. We haven't got a clue as to where he could be."

"Maybe we're closer than we think," Joe suggested.

Frank looked thoughtful. "You may have a point," he said. "Maybe we almost found Clarence and didn't know it. And maybe whoever kidnapped him is getting nervous."

"So where have you been looking?" Marcy asked.

"A few places around the station," Joe replied. "But maybe we haven't searched those places thoroughly enough."

"By the way," Marcy said, "I remembered something that might be of interest to you. The day before Clarence disappeared, he told me that he needed to talk to Matt Freeman. I don't know what about, but he seemed a little worked up over something. I arranged for Clarence and Freeman to get together Sunday morning, since I knew both of them would be in the studios that day."

"That's the morning Clarence vanished," Frank said. "I wonder if they ever had that talk?"

"I don't know," Marcy said. "But it's possible. Maybe you should ask Matt about it."

"Good idea," Frank said. "That is, if he's talking to us after the conversation my brother had with him last night."

"Hey," Joe said. "I was just doing my job. But maybe I did come on a little strong with him."

Frank rolled his eyes at his brother as they headed for the door of Marcy's office. "Well, I guess we'd better get back on the investigation. Thanks for the tip, Marcy."

"I wonder where Steve and Debbie are?" Joe asked, as the brothers headed down the hallway. "Weren't we going to talk to them today?"

"Yeah, but now I'm not sure we can spare the time," Frank said. "They probably wouldn't even listen to us. Anyway, we've got to get serious about this case. Finding Clarence is our top priority. We can't worry about Steve and Debbie."

Suddenly a piercing scream echoed up and down the WBPT corridors.

"It came from somewhere outside the building," Joe said.

"Let's go!" Frank exclaimed.

The brothers dashed out the back door. A baffled guard was standing outside the door, looking around for the source of the screams.

"Keep watching the exit!" Frank yelled to the guard. "We'll take care of this."

The scream sounded again.

"It's coming from over here," Joe said, pointing around the corner of the building.

The Hardys raced in the direction of the scream and then came to an abrupt halt as they rounded the corner.

The first thing Frank saw was Steve Burke, standing next to the building and looking upward helplessly. Then, as Frank followed Steve's gaze, he saw Debbie. She was hanging by her hands from the rain gutter that ran just under the jutting edge of the building's roof, two stories above the ground. She was dangling next to the first of three long windows that faced out onto the rear parking lot. It looked to Frank as though she had climbed up the drain spout that ran down one corner of the building and tried to make her way along the gutter to the windows. She had a tight grip on the gutter with both of her hands, but Frank knew that her weight would soon cause it to come loose.

"Help me, someone," Debbie gasped, looking down at the hard asphalt below.

The gutter made a cracking sound as part of it came loose from the roof, and Debbie screamed again.

# 10 Clarence Speaks

"You've got to get her down!" Steve yelled. "She could be killed!"

"I think I saw a ladder on the ground next to the back door," Joe said. He ran back toward the door and found the tall aluminum ladder, splattered with brightly colored splotches of paint, lying next to the wall. Joe grabbed it and dragged it back around to the side of the building, where Debbie was dangling helplessly.

"Hurry!" Steve shouted. "I don't know how much longer she can hold on."

"Take it easy, Steve," Joe replied. "We'll get her down."

With Frank's help, Joe mounted the ladder against the side of the building next to Debbie.

Frank grabbed the sides of the ladder and held it steady while Joe scaled it rapidly. The younger Hardy came up beneath Debbie and grabbed her under the arms. The ladder was just tall enough for him to get a grip on her.

"Okay, I've got you," Joe told Debbie. "Let go of the gutter, and I'll lower you to the top rung of the ladder."

"Let go of the gutter?" Debbie shouted. "I'll fall!"

There was another cracking noise, and the gutter sagged even lower.

"You'll fall if you don't let go," Joe said urgently. "You're just going to have to trust me to hold on to you."

Debbie gave Joe a look that was anything but trusting. But after glancing back up at the sagging gutter, she nodded. She let go of the gutter, and as she did, it finally gave way and crashed to the pavement. Joe lowered Debbie onto the upper rungs of the ladder. With his help, she made her way gradually back down the ladder and onto the ground. By the time she reached the bottom, she was trembling.

"You'd both better have a good explanation for this," Frank said sharply.

"Or what?" Steve said. "Are you gonna send a note to our parents?"

"We were engaged in perfectly legitimate detective activities," Debbie said defensively. "I was performing a surveillance operation."

"Surveillance?" Joe asked incredulously. "Of what?"

"Ted Whalen's office," Debbie said in a challenging tone. "You want to make something out of it?"

"Oh, no," Frank said with a groan. "You're not still on Ted Whalen's case, are you?"

"We've never been off it," Steve said. "He's clearly the kidnapper, and he has to be watched."

"So Debbie climbed up the drainpipe," Joe said, "grabbed the gutter to get a better look in Ted's window, and got stuck."

Debbie shrugged. "It could happen to anyone."

"So why does it always happen to you guys?" Joe asked.

"Well?" Steve asked Debbie, ignoring Joe's comment. "Did you find anything? What was going on in Ted's office?"

"Uh, nothing, actually," Debbie said. "I didn't get a chance to look. I was too busy trying not to fall off the gutter."

"Oh, that's great," Steve said. "All that work for nothing."

"Uh-oh," Frank said. "Look who's coming."

A small crowd of people, apparently drawn by Debbie's screaming, was coming around the corner from the parking lot. At the head of the crowd, flanked by his hulking bodyguards, was Ted Whalen. The station manager's face was red with anger, and he was clenching his fists.

"Oh, no," Steve said, turning to run. "If that guy gets hold of us, we're history."

"We'd better make ourselves scarce," Debbie whispered. She and Steve took off around the other side of the building.

"Think we should join them?" Joe asked his brother. "Or should we stay here and explain the situation to Ted?"

"Get serious," Frank said, hurrying after Steve and Debbie.

Frank and Joe followed them around the building and went back inside through the front door. In the lobby, they paused a moment.

"Well, what now?" Joe asked.

"I think we should pick up where we left off," Frank said, "and pay a visit to Matt Freeman. We've been so sidetracked by Steve and Debbie that we haven't had time to take our suspects seriously. And I think that Freeman heads the list."

"Right you are, bro. Lead the way," Joe said.

Freeman's office was near Studio A, not far from Marcy Simons's office. When the Hardys poked their heads inside, however, Freeman gave them a look that said they weren't welcome.

"We need to ask you just a few more questions, Mr. Freeman," Frank said. "Then we'll let you alone."

"I thought I told you kids to go play your detective games somewhere else," Freeman said, scowling.

"It's really important that we talk to you, Mr. Freeman," Joe said.

Freeman looked at the Hardys for a moment.

97

"Oh, all right," he said finally. "You get precisely two more questions. But only because Marcy asked me to cooperate with you guys."

"Great," Joe said. "Marcy told us that you were supposed to have a talk with Clarence Kellerman on Sunday morning. Did Clarence ever show up?"

"No," Freeman replied. "Marcy sweet-talked me into meeting with Clarence at nine o'clock Sunday morning, but he never got here. I wasn't thrilled, because I like to sleep late on Sundays and I went out of my way to be here for our talk. If he hadn't vanished that day, I would have really bawled him out the next time I saw him."

"What was he going to talk to you about?" Frank asked. "Any idea?"

"How would I know?" Freeman snapped. "He never got here. Though I think I have an idea."

"What do you think it was about?" Joe asked.

"Sorry," Freeman said. "You've already asked your two questions. Now go away and let me get back to work."

"You haven't answered the second question yet," Frank pointed out quietly. "When you do, we'll get out of here."

Freeman sighed. "Oh, all right. There was a staff party on Friday night, and I guess I got a little talkative. I said some nasty things about the way Clarence ran his show and indicated that I could do a better job. A few of Clarence's friends overheard what I said and must have told him about it the next day. I guess he just wanted to confront me with it. I was even ready to apologize. But he didn't bother to show up."

"Maybe he couldn't make it to your meeting," Joe suggested. "Maybe somebody had already arranged for him to disappear."

"Yeah, sure," Freeman said. "I still think Clarence is pulling a fast one. And now I'd like to remind you that I've answered your two questions."

"Yes, you have," Frank said. "We were just leaving."

The Hardys left Freeman's office and wandered down the hallway. Once they were out of earshot, Frank said, "Something seems funny about that story."

"I know what you mean," Joe said. "If Clarence was kidnapped before his meeting with Freeman at nine in the morning, what was he doing in the station during the home-shopping show that afternoon?"

"I don't know," Frank said. "Freeman didn't look like he was lying."

"Well, somebody's lying," Joe said. "Maybe—"

"Hey, guys," said a familiar voice. Frank and Joe turned to see Steve Burke heading down the hallway toward them. "I've got an idea I want you two to hear."

Frank scowled. "Thanks, Steve, but Joe and I are discussing some ideas of our own right now."

"Yeah," Joe said. "Why don't you go tell your idea to Debbie? I'm sure she'll want to hear it."

"Oh, I want to apologize for Debbie," Steve said.

"She's been messing everything up. I have all these great ideas and she steals them."

"Sure, Steve," Frank said. "If it weren't for Debbie, you'd have solved the case by now."

"I'm glad you see it my way, Frank," Steve said with a grin. "I'm going to need some help with this idea of mine, and I figure you guys can't mess it up any more than Debbie would."

"Gee, thanks, Steve," Joe said. "But not right—"

Joe was interrupted by a crackling sound from a loudspeaker set high on one wall of the corridor. The static was followed by the booming sound of a human voice.

"Help!" the voice shouted. "It's Clarence. Get me out of here! I'm locked up in the ba—"

# 11 All Roads Lead Down

As suddenly as it had begun, the mysterious crackling on the loudspeaker went away, and with it, Clarence's voice.

"That was Clarence!" Joe cried. "Where was his voice coming from? It must have been right here in the building."

"Come on," Frank said, grabbing his brother's shoulder. "We've got to find out where the microphone for the system is located."

"Marcy will know," Joe said.

The brothers began to run down the hall toward Marcy's office. Steve Burke yelled after them, "Hey, don't you want to hear my idea?"

"Later, Steve!" Joe shouted. "We've finally got a real clue to Clarence's whereabouts."

As the Hardys rounded the corner, they saw Marcy Simons bolting out of her office. "Did you hear it?" she asked them.

"You bet we did," Frank said. "Where's the microphone for those speakers? That must be where Clarence is."

"There's one in the newsroom," Marcy said, "but I'm sure there are others. In fact, there are probably microphones all over the building."

Frank's face fell. "Then we've still got quite a search ahead of us."

"Maybe not," Joe said. "Marcy, show us the newsroom. Maybe we can find some kind of clue there."

Marcy took them to the newsroom, a spacious area lined with desks and filing cabinets. Frank noticed several reporters sitting at their desks in front of computer terminals. But instead of tapping out news stories or talking on the telephone, the reporters were talking excitedly with one another about Clarence's mysterious broadcast. In one corner of the room was a handheld microphone that was propped up on a stand.

"This microphone is attached to the P.A.," said Marcy, "but I don't see any sign of Clarence around here."

"Neither do I," Frank said. "I guess that would have been too easy. Still, it's good to know that Clarence is still alive."

"Right," Joe said. "Now we know for sure that Clarence is in the building."

"Maybe there's a blueprint somewhere that shows where the other microphones are," Frank suggested. "When was this P.A. system put in, anyway?"

"Years and years ago," Marcy said. "I doubt that there's any kind of blueprint or chart showing where the outlets are, but I'll take a look around." She headed back out into the hallway, leaving the brothers in the newsroom.

"What was it that Clarence said over the loud-speaker?" Joe asked. "That he was 'locked' some-where? Something like that?"

"He was 'locked in the ba—,' but he didn't get the whole word out," Frank said.

"Maybe he's locked in the bathroom," Joe said.

"No," Frank said. "It was a long *a*, like 'bay.'"

"Locked in the Bayport studios?" Joe suggested.

"How about locked in the basement?" Frank said.

Joe snapped his fingers. "Right, the basement. Where we found Steve and Debbie yesterday. But we've already looked there."

"It's a big basement," Frank said. "And it was pretty dark down there. We didn't really get the chance to search it thoroughly."

"We also got sidetracked by Steve and Debbie and the smoke," Joe added. "Do you think the kidnapper will try to stop us again if we start snooping around the basement a second time?"

"That's a chance we'll have to take," Frank said grimly.

Marcy reappeared in the newsroom. "I don't know if this will help, but one of the engineers tells me that there used to be a switchboard for the P.A. system in the basement. He didn't know if it was still working or not, and he wasn't even sure where it was, but it might still be there."

Joe's face lit up. "This is beginning to fall into place."

Frank nodded. "Everything's pointing toward the basement. Let's get back down there."

"Thanks, Marcy," Joe said as the brothers left the newsroom. "We'll let you know how things go."

"I hope you've still got that key to the basement," Frank said, as they headed down the hall. "I don't want to get locked in there again. And we might need it to get inside."

Joe patted the pocket of his jeans. "It's right here," he said with a grin. "I had a feeling we might need it."

When they reached the basement door, it was already open. And as they started down the stairs, they met Fred Dunlap coming up from below, a big cardboard box in his arms.

"Hi, guys," Fred said, edging past the Hardys on the stairs. He flashed them a big smile. "Glad to see you're still hard at work."

"Hi, Mr. Dunlap," Frank said. "What's in the box?"

"Oh, just merchandise for our show," Fred replied. "We keep all our stuff downstairs so we don't clutter up the studio."

104

"You wouldn't happen to know if there's an old microphone or switchboard downstairs someplace, would you?" Joe asked.

"Something that might be part of the P.A. system in this building," Frank added.

"Does this have something to do with Clarence's voice coming over the intercom?" Fred asked excitedly. "I heard that. Really weird. Do you think Clarence is still around here?"

"He must be," Joe said. "How else could he have been talking over the P.A.?"

"You're right," Fred said. "Yeah, I think I remember seeing some electronic stuff in the northwest corner downstairs. You might want to take a look."

"We will," Joe said. "Thanks a lot."

As Fred Dunlap disappeared through the door at the top of the stairs, Frank looked after him for a moment. "I wonder why he carries his own stuff up the stairs. He's a producer, and a host, after all. You'd think he'd have somebody to do that for him."

"Maybe it's one of Ted Whalen's cost-cutting measures," Joe said. "Let the producers and hosts do all the work."

"I guess so," Frank said. "Come on. Let's find that intercom."

The Hardys were pleased to see that lights were on in the basement. Fluorescent lamps hanging close to the ceiling provided lighting throughout the room. The boxes at the foot of the stairs had been rearranged to reveal a light switch that the Hardys had not noticed before.

"So that's where the light switch is," Joe said.

"Somebody must have gone to a lot of trouble to hide it from us the last time we were down here," Frank said.

In one corner of the room the Hardys found boxes piled up in front of the wall. Joe pulled one of the boxes off the pile and peered into the space behind it.

"There's something set into the wall back here," he reported. "But I can't make out what it is."

"Then we'll have to move these boxes," Frank said.

One by one, the Hardys moved the boxes away from the wall. Soon, the Hardys had revealed the structure that was set into the wall.

"It's the switchboard," Joe said, pulling the last box out of the way. "And here's the microphone!"

He bent over and picked the microphone up off the floor. It was attached to the switchboard at the end of a coiled wire.

Frank took the microphone and tapped it gently against one of the boxes. In the distance, he heard the sound of his soft tap magnified by the P.A. system.

"It's live," Joe said. "This must be the microphone Clarence used to send his message."

"We don't know that for sure," Frank replied. "Marcy said that there might be microphones all over the building."

"But why would this one still be on?" Joe asked, indicating a switch on the switchboard next to the microphone cable that was toggled to the ON position.

"That is strange," Frank agreed. "But if Clarence used this microphone, where is he now?"

"I don't know," Joe said. "Hey, Clarence! Are you around here someplace?"

"I don't hear anybody answering," Frank said. "Which doesn't mean—"

Suddenly the brothers heard a thin, weak voice. It sounded as if it was coming from inside one of the boxes. And it was identical to the voice they had heard on the loudspeaker.

"I'm right here. Help me before it's too late," the voice called.

"Clarence!" Joe shouted. He and Frank darted around through the piles of boxes stacked on the floor, looking in every nook they came across.

Then, as Joe reached another stack of boxes, he saw a man in a tailored blue suit. He grabbed him by the wrist and shouted to his brother, "Frank! I've got him. It's Clarence!"

# 12 Going Astray

Frank ran to his brother's side just as the blue-suited figure turned around.

"I'm not Clarence," said the man with the familiar brown mustache.

"No," Frank said. "You're Fred Dunlap."

"Have been all my life." Fred chuckled.

Joe's shoulders sagged in disappointment. "And I thought I'd found Clarence! Sorry, Fred."

"I'm sorry I'm not Clarence," Fred said. "What made you think I was?"

"We heard Clarence's voice coming from some-where near these boxes," Frank said. "Didn't you hear it, too?"

"No," Fred said. "I just came back down here to get some more merchandise."

"Maybe you can help us find Clarence," Joe said. "He's got to be in these boxes somewhere. That's where we heard his voice coming from."

"Sure, I'll be happy to give you a hand," Fred offered. "Where do you want to start looking?"

"Anywhere," Frank said. "There are tons of boxes and props down here where Clarence could be stuck. I don't even know where to begin looking."

"I'll start over here." Fred walked over to the far corner of the room.

While Fred Dunlap was working his way through the boxes and props in one corner of the room, Frank and Joe began looking in another. At first they searched the boxes and props systematically, but when no clues to Clarence's whereabouts surfaced, they became more and more frantic. Joe started to toss items around wildly.

"Take it easy," Frank cautioned. "We're more likely to find him if we do this carefully. If you start throwing things around like that, you might end up burying Clarence instead of unburying him."

Joe took a deep breath. "All right, I'll slow down. But we're so close."

"It's about time we were close," Frank said. "Until now, all of our clues to Clarence have seemed to lead to dead ends."

"Do you have any idea where that voice came from?" Joe asked. "If we can pin down the source, we'll have Clarence."

"I'm stumped," Frank said, shaking his head.

"There are too many echoes down here. It could have come from anywhere."

The Hardys continued to search through boxes and old trunks. But after working for an hour, they came up empty.

"I'm afraid I'm ready to give up, boys," Fred announced. "I don't see any sign of Clarence, and I've got a show to put on."

"Oh, right," Joe said. "Thanks for the help, anyway."

"I'm just going to grab my stuff and head back upstairs."

"By the way," Frank said, "where do you keep this merchandise of yours, anyway?"

Fred smiled. "Over there," he said with a vague wave of his hand. "Where it won't get in anybody's way."

"Maybe we can take a look at it later," Joe said with a laugh. "The thought of all that gold in one place makes my heart beat faster."

"You don't really want to see it," Fred said. "Just a lot of dull boxes. Like the rest of this basement."

"Sounds pretty boring, all right," Frank said.

Fred Dunlap said goodbye to the Hardys, grabbed a box, and headed up the stairs.

"I guess maybe we should call it quits, too," Frank said with a sigh. "Searching this basement may be too much work for the two of us. We need help."

"I guess you're right," Joe said. "Maybe we can get some of the building guards to pitch in."

"Come on," Frank said, walking Joe back to the stairs. "Let's tell Marcy what's happened and let her find some people who can search the basement."

On the way out, Joe noticed the locked wire cage his brother had stumbled into on their first trip into the basement. In the brighter light, he could now see what was on the other side: stacks of boxes mostly covered with thick tarpaulin. The boxes had the initials HSE printed on the side.

"This must be where Fred and Al keep the merchandise for the 'Home-Shopping Extravaganza,'" Joe said. "That would explain the initials." He gazed at the boxes. "Sure is a lot of stuff," he commented. "I wonder where they get it all."

"Must buy it wholesale," Frank said, "in large quantities. This looks like enough merchandise to keep them going for months at a time."

"Probably the cheapest way to do it," Joe said.

"I wonder why they keep it locked away in this cage?"

"Probably afraid it'll get stolen," Joe said. "All those gold chains must be pretty valuable."

Frank grinned. "At nineteen ninety-five apiece, I'm surprised they don't have an armed guard around them."

The brothers laughed. Then they started back up the stairs.

"I don't believe any of this," Joe said, as they reached the top of the stairs and stepped into the hallway. "We were in the same room with Clarence

111

—he even talked to us—and we still couldn't find him. Are we losing our detective touch or what?"

"I've been thinking about that," Frank said. "Has it occurred to you that somebody might be leading us on a false trail?"

"What do you mean?" Joe asked.

"Maybe Clarence isn't in the basement at all," Frank said. "Maybe somebody just wants us to think that Clarence is in the basement so that we'll stay away from the place where Clarence really is."

"But you heard his voice yourself," Joe protested. "We weren't imagining that. And when Clarence spoke over the loudspeaker, he said that he was trapped in the 'ba—,' which sounds like he's in the basement to me."

"What if that wasn't Clarence?"

"Not Clarence?" Joe said in a puzzled tone. "It was Clarence's voice. I've been listening to Clarence for years on TV, and I'd know his voice anywhere. Clarence has the kind of voice that's easy to recognize."

"Clarence has a pretty distinctive voice, all right," Frank said. "It's so distinctive—"

"Yoo hoo," called a female voice from down the hall. "It's me again."

Frank turned in the direction of the voice. "Oh, hello, Debbie," he said.

Joe noticed his brother's lack of enthusiasm. "What are you and Steve up to now?" he asked suspiciously.

112

Debbie smiled slyly. "Well, we got hold of this small TV camera that nobody was using—"

"As though we weren't already in enough hot water," Joe interrupted.

"And we put it in Ted Whalen's office," Debbie finished.

"You did what?" Frank roared. "Are you out of your minds? Do you know what will happen if Ted Whalen finds out you're spying on him?"

"Oh, he'll never know," Debbie said, trying to reassure the Hardys. "We stuck the camera in with all of those televisions he keeps on the wall of his room. With all that electronic equipment there, he'll never notice another piece."

"What are you going to do with this camera?" Joe asked. "Make home videos of your close friend Ted?"

"That's the great part," Debbie said excitedly. "Steve has figured out a way to patch the camera into the closed circuit TV system here at the station and watch it on one of the monitors. I have to admit that Steve actually does have a talent or two."

"I don't believe I'm hearing this," Frank said. "You guys are actually tampering with the TV system here at the station?"

"Don't worry," Debbie said cheerfully. "We know what we're doing. Now we'll be able to watch every move that Ted Whalen makes. When he reveals where Clarence is hidden away, we'll be listening to every word."

"Where's Steve now?" Joe asked. "Has he already finished doing all of this?"

"He's in the engineering room next to Studio A," Debbie said. "He's adjusting one of the monitors in there while the engineers aren't looking. Any minute now, we'll be able to get a look into Ted's office."

"Come on," Frank said, running toward the studio. "It might not be too late to stop him."

"Nothing's blown up yet," Joe said, hurrying after his brother.

"I don't understand," Debbie said. "Why do you want to stop Steve? I thought you were interested in finding Clarence."

The Hardys didn't stop to answer Debbie as they raced toward the studio. But before Frank and Joe could reach their destination, they saw Marcy Simons pull open the door to the engineering room from the inside and stagger out into the hallway. A puff of black smoke followed her out. She was coughing loudly.

"Thank goodness you're here," she gasped when she saw the Hardys racing toward her. "You've got to do something, quick. The engineering room's about to explode!"

# 13 Hidden Camera

"What do you mean, explode?" Frank asked. "Is something on fire?"

"The wires are burning . . . melting. . . . Everything could catch," Marcy said. "Get the fire extinguisher. Quick!"

Frank ran to the glass case on the wall, reached through the remains of the glass that he had shattered the day before, and grabbed the fire extinguisher. He shook it to reassure himself that it was full, then ran to the door of the engineering room and pushed his way inside.

The smoke was pouring out of a bank of TV monitors on one wall. Frank sprayed the fire extinguisher at the source of the fire, and after a few moments the smoke began to clear.

"Uh, hi, Frank," the older Hardy heard a nervous voice say below him. He looked down and saw Steve sitting on the floor in front of the monitors, several tools at his side.

"Guess it really wasn't much of a fire," Steve said, getting up off the floor. "Thanks for putting it out, though."

"Let me guess," Frank said coolly. "Did you have something to do with this, Steve?"

"Well, I must have put two wrong wires together," Steve said uneasily. "There were a few sparks and then suddenly all this smoke. Everything's okay now, though."

"Yeah, sure," Joe said, coming up behind Frank. "You could have burned the whole building down."

On the opposite side of the room, a pair of engineers watched the three teens closely. One was the young brown-haired engineer Frank and Joe had seen the day before. The other was a middle-aged man with thinning gray hair.

"What's going on, anyway?" the man asked. "Were you the ones who caused that fire? What are you doing in here?"

"Our friend Steve will be doing the explaining," Joe said. "Right, Steve?"

Suddenly the brown-haired engineer looked up at the bank of TV screens in front of her and cried out, "Hey, what is this? That's not supposed to be on the air. Don't we have a game show scheduled for this half hour?"

The older engineer turned to look at the screen,

too, as did Frank, Joe, and Steve. Debbie Hertzberg, who had just entered the room, peered over their shoulders.

On each of the seven televisions was the same image: the inside of Ted Whalen's office, with Whalen sitting behind his spacious desk, leaning back comfortably in his padded chair.

"Well, if it isn't Ted the Tyrant," said the brown-haired engineer. "What's he doing on there? We don't have a feed from his office, do we?"

"Not that I know of," the other engineer replied.

"Isn't that the picture from the camera we put in Ted's room?" Debbie whispered to Steve.

"Uh, yeah," Steve said. "I think it is." He leaned forward and talked to the two engineers. "That's not actually on the air, is it?"

"You bet it is," said the brown-haired engineer, staring at the image in astonishment. "Somehow this picture has been patched directly into the broadcast signal. Television viewers throughout the Bayport broadcasting area are watching this right along with us."

"We'd all better run for our lives when Ted figures out what's happened," the second engineer said.

"So that's what that red cable did," Steve said. "I'll have to remember that next time."

As the people in the engineering room watched Ted on the monitor, the station manager picked up a sandwich from the desk in front of him, started to take a bite from it, and spilled lettuce and mayon-

117

naise down his shirt and tie. Several of the workers in the engineering room laughed and clapped, and someone let out a loud whistle.

With an exasperated expression, Whalen looked down at the mess he had made. Then he glanced up at the banks of television screens on his wall, and his expression began to change. His jaw dropped and his eyes grew wide. The lettuce and mayonnaise dribbled slowly from his tie to the top of his desk.

"What do you think he's looking at?" Steve asked.

"Himself," Joe replied. "On TV."

The brown-haired engineer smiled. "Maybe we shouldn't cut this off the air after all."

"Yeah," said the older engineer. "Sure beats our regular programming. Old Ted's never looked better."

Ted Whalen, staring straight at the TV screen, began to flush with anger.

Then he said, in a low and menacing tone, "I'm going to *kill* those kids!"

"You don't suppose he means us, do you?" Debbie asked.

"I think we'd better get moving," Frank said to Joe.

"Right," Joe said. "It looks like things are about to get pretty nasty around here."

Frank and Joe stepped out of the engineering room and into the hallway as quickly as they could.

118

"Now, where were we?" Joe asked.

"We were talking about Clarence and whether that was really his voice over the intercom," Frank said.

"It might be time to ask a few people where they were when that message was broadcast," Joe said.

"Here comes one of them now." Frank pointed down the hallway. Matt Freeman was striding toward them.

"Where are you headed, Matt?" Joe asked. "You look like you're in a hurry."

"I've got a special edition of 'The Four O'Clock Scholar' to host this evening," Matt replied. "And, as I recall, your brother Frank is a contestant on it."

"Oh, right!" Frank exclaimed. "The championship tournament is tonight, and I'm on the team. I was planning on doing a little cramming before the show. I haven't had a chance to study since Sunday."

"Calm down," Joe said. "You were great on Sunday, and you'll probably blow them all away tonight."

"If you two don't mind," Matt said, "I've got to get moving. Good luck to you." He continued down the hallway toward the studio.

"Listen," Frank said. "I've got to start getting ready for the show, too. You go talk to Marcy Simons and tell her to have the basement searched for Clarence."

"You still think he's down there?" Joe asked.

"I'm not sure," Frank said. "But we have to cover all the bases."

"Okay," Joe said. "Anything else?"

"Just keep trying to find Clarence," Frank said. "I'll compare notes with you as soon as the show is over."

Frank turned and headed for the greenroom, leaving Joe alone in the hallway. After watching his brother go, Joe walked to Marcy Simons's office.

Marcy was startled when Joe told her about hearing Clarence in the basement, and she agreed to send a pair of guards down to search. She then excused herself, saying she also had to get ready for "The Four O'Clock Scholar."

Joe wandered back out into the hallway. Well, it's up to me now, he thought. I've got to figure this one out on my own.

Joe found an empty office and settled down into a comfortable-looking chair. It felt good to sit down after a day of running around looking for Clarence.

He remembered what Frank had started to say earlier about Clarence's voice. It was so distinctive that—what? What had Frank been about to say?

That someone could easily have imitated Clarence's voice?

Sure, thought Joe. That made sense. What if the voice they had heard over the loudspeaker and in the basement was someone doing a Clarence Kellerman impression?

So who did a Clarence Kellerman impression?

"Hello, everybody," Joe said out loud, trying to

make his voice sound as much like the quiz show host's as possible. "It's your old buddy Clarence!"

Nah, he thought, with a shudder. That was a lousy Clarence Kellerman impression.

But maybe somebody who made his living talking on television could do a better one. Maybe somebody like—

Joe stood up abruptly, almost knocking over the chair as he did. He realized he knew who did a great Clarence Kellerman impression. Joe had heard Fred Dunlap do it just the previous morning, on the set of the Home-Shopping Extravaganza.

And Fred had been in the basement the second time they had heard Clarence's voice. He could have made it sound as though Clarence were hidden away somewhere in the stacks of boxes.

Joe raced back out into the hallway—and froze. Where were Fred and Al anyway? He always saw them in the hallway or on the stairs or in the studio, but he had no idea where their office was.

Joe ducked his head into an office and asked the man who sat at the desk where he could find the Dunlaps.

"I just saw them outside," the man said. "On the loading dock down at the end of this hall. They're unloading a bunch of merchandise that just came in."

Why would the Dunlaps be outside unloading their own merchandise? Joe wondered as he headed for the dock. Shouldn't they have other people do that job for them?

He and Frank had seen Fred carrying boxes up from the basement. Why did the Dunlaps handle the merchandise entirely by themselves?

Maybe, thought Joe, they don't want anybody else to see it. Maybe there's something funny about the boxes and boxes of merchandise that the Dunlaps kept in the basement.

And maybe, just maybe, Clarence had gotten too close a look at the merchandise. . . .

Joe threw open the door to the loading dock. There was a large truck backed up to the dock, but nobody was in sight around it. Joe walked up to the open, rear door of the truck and looked inside. There were piles of boxes in the truck, similar to the boxes he and Frank had seen stacked in the basement.

Joe stepped inside the truck and took a closer look. A couple of boxes were marked HSE, but most were marked with the names of Bayport area stores. Were these the places where Fred and Al bought their merchandise? Joe wondered. Hadn't Fred said on the show that they bought their merchandise wholesale, to keep the prices down?

Joe cautiously opened the lid on one box. Inside were all types of gold chains, like the ones that Fred had been hawking on the show the previous morning. The box next to it contained assorted jewelry, which had been tossed carelessly into the box.

This stuff didn't look as if it had been bought wholesale, Joe thought. This looked like—

"Can I help you?" said a voice. Joe spun around to see Fred and Al Dunlap staring into the truck.

"Where'd you get this stuff?" Joe asked the brothers. "Where does it all come from?"

"What business is it of yours?" Fred asked. "I thought you kids were looking for Clarence Kellerman, not a good buy on gold chains."

"This stuff is stolen, isn't it?" Joe snapped. "That's why you never let anybody get near your merchandise or unlock your truck for you. Clarence found out that this stuff was stolen and that's why he's missing now, right?"

Fred and Al exchanged glances. "This kid is pretty smart," Al said with a scowl. "And his brother, too. Real sharp detectives."

"You guys are running a fencing operation right out of this station, aren't you?" Joe went on. "You sell the stuff to the viewers of your show, who never suspect they're buying stolen merchandise. You must get this stuff from every petty crook in town."

"That's about the size of it," Al said. "We're the hottest fences in Bayport. And the thieves don't even have to come to us. We come to them, with this handy truck."

"And you've been trying to get rid of me and my brother all along, not to mention Steve and Debbie," Joe continued. "You dropped that camera on us, didn't you? And which one of you tried to knock me off the catwalk Sunday evening?"

Fred gestured to Joe and smiled. "This kid really is smart, Al."

123

"You even locked all four of us in the basement and tried to asphyxiate us with smoke before we discovered anything important," Joe said.

"Believe me," Fred said, "it wasn't much fun knocking those two other kids over the head with a crowbar after we'd turned out the lights on them in the basement. Fortunately, they never shut up for even a second, so it was easy to find them in the dark."

"You know," Al added, "this kid is so smart, I think I'll give him a little present." He reached inside his pocket and pulled out a gun.

"I guess you've solved the mystery after all, kid," Al said, pointing the gun at Joe. "Too bad. 'Cause it looks like your detective career is over."

# 14  Clarence Returns

Joe looked around desperately. No one else was in sight. Frank, Marcy, and Matt—and even Steve and Debbie—were all getting ready for "The Four O'Clock Scholar." That left Joe alone on the loading dock with a pair of armed criminals.

For the first time in days, Joe wouldn't have minded seeing Steve and Debbie show up.

"Well, kid," Al Dunlap said, waving the gun, "are you coming quietly? Or do we have to carry you?"

"I'm coming," Joe said, stepping out of the back of the truck. "Where exactly are we going?"

"Just follow me," Fred said. "Al will be right behind you, so don't try anything funny."

Al pushed the gun into his jacket pocket. "It's still aimed at you," he said. "I don't mind blowing a hole in this jacket if I have to."

"You've probably got a box full of brand-new jackets in the basement," Joe said.

"How'd you guess?" Fred said with a laugh. "They were real cheap, too."

There was a guard stationed inside the door. Joe tried to alert the man to his problem through his facial expression, but the guard was too absorbed in a paperback novel to notice. Al Dunlap, noticing what Joe was up to, poked the gun into the small of Joe's back.

Fred walked quickly past Studio A and opened the door to the staircase leading to the second level. Joe followed him up the stairs. A moment later they came to the door marked Studio A Catwalks. Fred opened it up and beckoned for Joe to follow him inside.

"So this is where you put Clarence," Joe said. "Frank and I must have come close to finding him on Sunday, when we came up here."

"Yeah," Al said. "Fortunately, Fred was up here at the time and managed to distract you by knocking you over the railing before you could get too close."

"And that's why you lured us to the basement," Joe said. "It was as far away from Clarence as we could get."

"My brother does a pretty good impression of

Clarence," Al said in a satisfied tone. "The one he did for you in the basement really had you going."

"Keep it down," Fred ordered. "We don't want anybody in the studio to hear you."

Joe followed Fred into the dimly lit catwalk area. With Al prodding him from behind with the gun, he made his way across to the opposite wall, where a dark-colored canvas had been laid across an object on the floor.

Fred removed the canvas with a flourish. Underneath was a tall, thin man. He had thick, wavy brown hair and was dressed in a brown, double-breasted suit. He was bound head-to-toe with ropes and gagged with a white handkerchief.

"Clarence," Joe whispered.

Clarence said something under his gag and made an effort to sit up.

"Be quiet, Clarence," Al whispered, "or we might forget to bring you breakfast tomorrow morning. You wouldn't like that, would you?"

Clarence looked up with wide eyes but said nothing.

"Now it's your turn, Joe," Fred said, taking hold of Joe's hands. "Put your hands behind your back, so that I can tie them up."

With Al still holding the gun on him, Joe stood quietly while Fred tied his wrists behind him with a length of rope. Then he sat down next to Clarence as Fred tied his legs and ankles and gagged his mouth.

Joe sat still as the ropes were tightened against his wrists, then watched as Fred stood up and surveyed his work. Al slipped the gun back into his pocket and began to walk away.

"We'll be back soon," Fred said. "We've finally decided where we're going to dump you guys. I hope you're ready for a long trip."

Joe watched as the Dunlaps walked back across the catwalks and through the door to the hallway. He could see the lights from the studio below and hear the sound of a crew putting up the set for "The Four O'Clock Scholar."

He turned and looked at Clarence. Clarence turned and looked at him.

Great detective work, thought Joe. I've finally found Clarence. Now who's going to find me?

Several hundred feet away, totally unaware of his brother's predicament, Frank Hardy was sitting on the sofa in the WBPT greenroom, preparing for the evening's contest by thumbing through the book his brother had left behind on Sunday.

"It won't do you any good, Hardy," Steve said. He was sprawled out in an easy chair nearby. "I'm getting my revenge tonight. I wasn't in my best form on Sunday, but this time I'm going to blow you away."

"Forget it, Steve," Debbie said, standing next to the sofa fastening a barrette in her hair. "Tonight I'm going to show the world how brilliant I really am—and I'm going to blow both of you away."

"That'll be the day," Steve retorted.

Frank sighed and put the book down. "I'm kind of distracted by the Clarence Kellerman case," he said. "I feel bad about leaving Joe to solve it by himself—at least until the show is over."

"It's time to get onstage," said Marcy Simons, stepping into the greenroom with her ever-present clipboard tucked under her arm. She led the two teams into Studio A and had a technician remind them how to use the electronic equipment at their seats. Looking up at the studio audience as he sat down, Frank spotted Callie, Iola, and Chet but saw no sign of Joe. Where could his brother be? he wondered. Could he have found an important clue leading to Clarence?

The technicians worked efficiently around the stage, and the camera operators set up the opening shot. Somebody did a brief countdown, and then the show was on the air. Matt Freeman began introducing himself to the audience.

Frank wasn't thinking about the show, however. He was thinking about the case. Where was Clarence Kellerman? If he wasn't in the basement, where was he? And who had fooled them into thinking he was in the basement in the first place?

Frank reminded himself that they *had* heard Clarence's voice in the basement. So either Clarence was there and they had been unable to find him or someone was imitating Clarence's voice.

Imitating Clarence's voice? Something clicked

when Frank thought about this. Who knew how to imitate Clarence's voice?

Suddenly Frank had a clear picture in his head of Fred Dunlap saying, "It's your old buddy, Clarence!" And Joe and I found Fred Dunlap in the basement right after we heard Clarence's voice, Frank thought. I've got to find Joe and tell him.

Frank stood up. He was about to rush out of the studio when, abruptly, he was aware that there was a camera on him and that Matt Freeman was scowling at him. Steve Burke grabbed the corner of Frank's jacket and pulled him back into his seat.

Great! Frank thought. I'm trapped on this quiz show while Clarence's kidnappers are running around the station with nobody to stop them. Except my brother. I wonder where Joe is right now?

Joe was barely more than thirty feet from where Frank was sitting in Studio A—thirty feet straight up. He had twisted himself around so that he could look over the edge of the catwalk and down into the studio below. Frank, Steve, and Debbie were sitting almost directly beneath him, giving him a perfect view of the top of their heads. He would have yelled to them for help, but the gag was stuffed tightly in his mouth.

Clarence had managed to turn himself so that his hands were next to Joe's hands. He reached out his fingers and tried to untie the rope around Joe's wrist.

Then Joe heard a jingling sound from only a few inches away. He looked down to see that some coins had fallen out of his pocket onto the catwalk. He squirmed around until the coins were directly under his nose.

Using the tip of his nose, he pushed a coin until it was on the very edge of the catwalk. Looking down on Frank, Steve, and Debbie far below, Joe pushed the coin over the edge.

It fell straight into Debbie's lap.

Joe saw Debbie look down at the unexpected gift, then look up at the ceiling above her. Joe moved his head around frantically, trying to catch her attention, but it was either too dark in the catwalks for her to see him, or she was blinded by the glare of the overhead spotlights.

Debbie turned to Steve and then Frank, trying to indicate to them that a coin had fallen into her lap. But neither of them paid any attention to her.

Joe saw that the quiz show had already begun. Although he couldn't quite make out the questions being asked, he could see Frank reaching out to press his buzzer. Turning away from the action below, Joe went back to the task of getting himself and Clarence untied and away from the catwalks before Al and Fred came back.

He began working at Clarence's ropes this time. After a while, he could feel the ropes around Clarence's wrists begin to give. As quickly as possible Joe worked at the delicate operation until the knots came loose. Finally the ropes fell away.

Clarence rubbed his wrists for a second. Then he pulled the gag from his mouth.

"Whoooeee!" he announced. "Boy, is it good to be able to talk again!"

Joe made as much noise as he could under his gag to try to tell Clarence to take the cloth off.

"Oh, yeah," Clarence said. "Sorry, buddy. I sure didn't mean to leave you tied up any longer than I had to. Let me get that gag out of your mouth."

Clarence worked at the knot on Joe's gag until it came loose. Joe shook the cloth off his mouth and ran his tongue around his lips to wet them.

"Thanks, Clarence," Joe said with relief. "You don't know how long my brother and I have been looking for you."

"Well," Clarence said, "I'm glad somebody's been looking for me. I was beginning to think I was stuck up here for the rest of my life."

"Maybe we can call for help now," Joe said. "Hey, somebody!" he shouted. "Come up here and get us untied!"

"Hold off on the yelling for a minute," Clarence said. "That's a live show going on down there, and we don't want to interrupt them. It'll just take us a minute to get these ropes off, then we can go on down there ourselves."

"Okay," Joe said. "Maybe if you turned yourself around, you could get to the ropes on my legs."

"Good thinking," Clarence said. "Let me just wiggle myself over here for a minute."

Clarence squirmed along the catwalk, his legs

132

still tightly bound with ropes. He positioned himself next to Joe's legs and reached out to begin untying them.

But he had pushed himself a little too close to the edge of the catwalk. With a sudden cry of "Whoops!" Clarence tumbled abruptly over the edge.

Joe tried to grab Clarence, but his wrists were still partially tied. He saw Clarence reach for the edge of the catwalk as he fell, but the show host managed to grab a fistful of tangled cables instead. The cluster of cables began unraveling instantly under his weight, and within seconds Clarence found himself twisted up in them, still falling.

Clarence fell straight down into the studio below. Two-thirds of the way to the floor, the cable stopped unraveling and broke Clarence's fall. For a few seconds, he bounced at the end of the cable as if he were a human yo-yo. Then the bouncing stopped, and he found himself dangling in midair, in front of Matt Freeman, the studio audience, the contestants, and the crew, not to mention everybody who was watching "The Four O'Clock Scholar" at home.

Clarence looked down to see a camera pointed directly at him. At the realization that he was on the air, his eyes opened wide and a big smile lit up his face.

"Hello, everybody!" he proclaimed loudly. "You may not believe this, but it's your old buddy Clarence!"

# 15 Hostage!

Frank looked up and couldn't believe his eyes. Sure enough, there was Clarence Kellerman, host of "The Four O'Clock Scholar," swinging from the cable.

Frank looked around to catch the reaction of the others. The studio audience rose to its feet and began pointing and shouting. And the other contestants also stood up and stared at Clarence, forgetting that they were on television.

Even Matt Freeman sprang from his chair and shouted angrily, "I *knew* that Clarence was going to pull some cheap publicity stunt!"

Marcy Simons rushed into the middle of the studio. "This doesn't look like a publicity stunt to me," she said. "I think Clarence is really in trouble."

One of the studio engineers grabbed a stepladder and a pair of pliers and raced over to cut Clarence down. Meanwhile, Frank stared up into the recesses of the catwalks, trying to determine what was going on. He considered shouting to see if his brother was concealed somewhere in the shadows, but the noise in the studio was so loud that he knew he would never be heard.

"Something funny's going on here," Frank murmured.

"Yeah, it's hilarious," Steve said. "Did you see the way Clarence came bouncing down on that rope?"

"So is it all just a stunt?" Debbie asked. "Clarence really wasn't missing at all?"

"I'm not so sure about that," Frank said, slipping away from his seat. "I'm going to take a closer look upstairs."

"Hey!" Steve shouted. "You can't run out now. We're in the middle of the show."

"It doesn't look like there's going to be much of a show today," Frank said, hurrying out of the studio.

Could Joe have something to do with what had just happened? Frank wondered as he bounded up the stairs to the second floor.

As he neared the door to the catwalks, he saw Fred and Al Dunlap hurrying through it.

Frank wondered if they had seen Clarence fall

135

out of the catwalks, too. He decided it wasn't likely, since they had reached the catwalks before he did.

Waiting until Al let the door slam behind him, Frank silently opened it again and looked inside.

He saw Fred and Al standing in the middle of the catwalks, looking around in confusion. Joe was lying on the far side of the catwalk, partially bound with thick ropes.

"What happened to Clarence?" Fred asked his brother, looking in disbelief at the spot where the quiz show host had been lying. "Where did he go?"

"Uh-oh," Al said. "Look down there." He pointed below, into the studio. As he pointed, Frank realized that he was holding a gun.

"Hey," Fred said, looking up at Frank. "Who's that?"

"It's the other Hardy kid," Al said, pointing his gun at Frank. "Come on inside, kid. Join your brother."

"What have you done to Joe?" Frank asked, stepping the rest of the way through the door. "You haven't hurt him, have you?"

"No," Joe said. "I'm okay."

Frank slowly walked over toward the far end of the catwalk, where his brother was lying.

"Our cover's been blown," Fred said to his brother in a shaky voice. "We've got to get out of here—fast."

"We'll take that kid with us," Al said, pointing at Joe. "The other one can stay here. We only need one hostage."

Fred walked over to Joe, while Al kept his gun trained on Frank.

Joe squirmed as Fred untied the ropes around his legs and retied the bonds on his wrists.

Frank's mind was racing. He had to think of a plan to get them out of here—and fast.

"Get up," Fred ordered Joe.

When Joe had gotten to his feet, Fred led him back toward the door.

"Don't give us any trouble," Al said to Frank. "We just want your brother, so that nobody'll give us any hassle getting out of here."

"What's this all about?" Frank asked Joe. "What happened since I last saw you?"

"I'll tell you about it the next time I see you," Joe said. "And believe me, I will see you again."

"I wouldn't count on it, kid," Al said, pointing the gun at Joe's head. "You know too much. Way too much."

"So does this kid, now," Fred added, pointing at Frank. "What should we do about him?"

Al raised his gun toward Frank. The elder Hardy didn't wait to see what he was going to do with it. Instead, he turned and leaped off the edge of the catwalk onto the top of a tall camera boom he had noticed only a few feet below. He hit the camera with a hard thump, but managed to keep a grip on it as the boom lowered to the studio floor under his weight.

"What in the world . . . ?" Marcy Simons shouted as Frank let go of the boom and landed on the floor next to her. "Where did you come from?"

"I'll tell you later," Frank called out as he raced toward the studio door. "I've got an emergency to handle."

Frank rushed up the steps to the second floor just in time to see Fred and Al leading Joe around a corner. As Frank followed, he saw them open a door and disappear into a stairwell.

Frank tiptoed quietly after them down the stairs. On the first floor, the Dunlaps led Joe down a back hallway, threatened the guard at the door with the gun, and proceeded out onto the loading dock. By the time Frank got to the door, Al was pushing Joe into the back of a truck parked at the loading dock. Al slammed the doors and hurried into the passenger side of the truck. The engine roared to life, and the truck began to pull away, with Fred at the wheel.

Frank noticed a narrow platform jutting out from the bottom of the doors. He shot forward and leaped onto the platform just as the truck began to pick up speed. He grabbed the back door handle so that he wouldn't fall off.

The truck raced out of the parking lot and into the street, almost hurling Frank to the pavement. But he clung tightly to the door handle and managed to hang on.

The Dunlaps hadn't had time to padlock the door. Frank pulled on the handle, almost falling off the truck as he did, and opened the door. Just as the truck accelerated down an access ramp and onto the freeway, Frank eased himself around the side of the door and fell onto the floor of the truck.

Joe was lying amid piles of cardboard boxes, his arms still bound. He looked up at his brother. "What took you so long?" he asked with a smile.

"Got held up in traffic," Frank replied, climbing awkwardly back to his feet. "Let's get you untied."

As Frank began working at the ropes on Joe's wrists, he asked, "So what happened while I was gone? I see you decided that you could solve this case without my help."

"I did solve it," Joe said. "Even if I managed to get myself kind of tied up in the process."

"So what's all this stuff in these boxes?" Frank asked. "More merchandise for the 'Home-Shopping Extravaganza'?"

"Stolen merchandise," Joe said. "That's what Clarence discovered, and it's why the Dunlaps stashed him away in the catwalks, until they figured out what to do with him. It's why they stuffed me away in the catwalks, too."

"How do you like that?" Frank said. "The answer was staring us in the face all that time, and we didn't see it."

"Speak for yourself," Joe said. "I solved this mystery with the sheer brilliance of my deductive powers."

"Please," Frank said, rolling his eyes. "You're beginning to sound like Steve and Debbie. I'll have you know I figured out a thing or two myself while the show was on. Okay, I think I've just about got your arms untied.''

Suddenly the brakes on the truck squealed, and the vehicle came to an abrupt halt. The engine died away, and there was a slamming sound as someone exited the cab. Then the Hardys heard quick footsteps as someone walked hastily around to the back of the truck.

''I've got an idea,'' Frank whispered as he moved back behind a stack of boxes.

The doors, which Frank had carefully closed after he had fallen into the back of the truck, popped open. It was getting dark outside, but Frank could make out the menacing figure of Al Dunlap climbing into the truck. Dunlap pointed his gun at Joe and stepped closer to him.

''Okay, kid,'' Al said. ''This is the end of the line for you.''

# 16 Unexpected Rescue

At that moment, Frank lunged from behind the stack of boxes and grabbed Al Dunlap firmly around the waist. Frank slammed Dunlap against the wall of the truck. Dunlap tried to shout for help, but Frank had knocked the breath out of him.

He tried to aim his gun at Frank, but Frank managed to grasp Dunlap's wrist. He rammed Dunlap's hand several times against the wall, forcing him to release the gun. Then he grabbed Dunlap under the shoulders, pulled him forward, and shoved him out the back door. As Dunlap fell to the ground, his head struck a rock, and he sagged into unconsciousness.

Meanwhile, Joe had managed to shuffle off the

remainder of the ropes. He hurried to his feet and joined Frank by the back door.

"Come on," Joe said. "Let's get out of here before Dunlap Number Two realizes what's happened."

They both leaped out to the ground and looked around. The Dunlaps had pulled the truck off the highway and parked it on a dirt road surrounded by trees. The Hardys started to run back in the direction of the highway, but it was too late. Fred Dunlap came barreling around the truck with a second gun gripped in his hands. He pointed the gun at the Hardys.

He glanced down at his brother, then glared at Frank and Joe.

"I've had enough of you kids," Fred said in a low, menacing voice. "You've really fouled everything up. In fact, I'm going to take care of you right now!"

Suddenly Frank heard the sound of a car engine on the dirt road behind the truck. He turned and saw a car approaching about fifteen feet away. It was beginning to grow dark, and the car's high beams prevented Frank from seeing who was driving.

"Police detectives! Throw down your guns! We've got you surrounded!" shouted a voice through the car window.

"What?" Fred screamed, spinning in the direction of the car. "Get away from me! You can't stop us now!"

Dunlap fired the gun directly into one of the car's

headlights, causing the glass to shatter. He took aim at the other headlight, but before he could fire a second shot, Joe grabbed his arm and wrestled the gun out of his hand. Defeated, Dunlap sagged to the ground between the Hardys and sat with his head in his hands.

"We almost made it," he said, moaning. "We had such a great scheme going. Didn't have to pay for any of the merchandise. Had all that money coming in. And then Clarence messed everything up. Clarence . . . and the Hardys."

"I don't think he's going to be much trouble," Frank told Joe. "Keep an eye on him, though, while I check out these police detectives."

Frank walked up to the car with the shattered headlight and looked in the window. To his surprise, he saw Steve Burke in the driver's seat. Sitting next to him was Debbie Hertzberg.

Steve looked out of the window at Frank, a wide grin on his face. "We saw you riding out on the back of that truck—" Steve began.

"So we thought it might be a good idea to follow you," Debbie finished. "Hope you don't mind. Oh, and we called the real police, too. They should be here any minute."

Frank stared at the pair in amazement. "Well, I never thought I'd say it, but I'm glad to see you two. I've got to give you credit. What you just did really took a lot of guts."

"Hey," Steve said. "If you're going to be a great detective, you've got to have guts."

"You guys did all right, too," Debbie said with a big smile.

The next afternoon, Clarence Kellerman sat in an easy chair in Marcy Simons's office and beamed at Frank and Joe. Marcy was pouring coffee for the group.

"I guess you two are just about the best buddies a poor kidnapped quiz show host could have," Clarence declared with a big smile. "I don't know what I would have done without you. Gone off to that great TV studio in the sky, I guess."

"Fred and Al," Marcy Simons said, shaking her head in disbelief. "I never would have suspected them. All those years they've been selling stolen merchandise on their show, and nobody even knew."

"Well, I was suspicious," Clarence said, accepting the cup of coffee Marcy held out to him. "I've always wondered about those two. It was strange how they kept all those boxes of stuff locked away in that cage down in the basement where nobody else could get a close look at them. Never did trust those guys."

"What finally tipped you off?" Joe asked. "How did you find out that they really were crooks?"

"It was this ring they were getting ready to sell on their show last Sunday," Clarence said. "I stopped by the studio for a few minutes before my appointment with Matt Freeman, and Al and Fred had their merchandise already set up for the show. I thought

144

the ring looked awfully familiar. I picked it up and sure enough, it was my ex-wife's wedding ring. She had left it with me when we got divorced, and I'd kept it tucked away in a drawer for years. It was stolen a few months ago when my house was burglarized. You can imagine my surprise when it turned up on Fred and Al's show. It even had her initials inside."

"So did you accuse them of stealing your ring?" Frank asked.

"I sure did," Clarence said. "Next thing I knew, old Al had pulled a gun out of his pocket and was telling me to walk up to the catwalks nice and slow. Then they tied me up and left me there while they figured out what to do with me."

"I put guards at all the entrances," Marcy said, sipping her coffee. "That probably kept them from taking you out of the building."

"And it's a good thing you did that," Clarence said. "Those two were ready to do away with me for good. They just didn't want to do it inside the station, where they might get caught."

"What time did all that happen, Clarence?" Frank asked. "My brother and I had a lot of trouble figuring out exactly when you got kidnapped."

"It was right after I got in that morning, around nine o'clock," Clarence replied. "I headed straight for the studio and then zap! Everything went wrong."

"So Fred and Al were lying when they said they had seen Clarence at one in the afternoon," Joe said. "But Matt Freeman was telling the truth about Clarence missing their meeting."

"By the way," Marcy said, "Matt Freeman would like to apologize for all the nasty things he said about you Friday night."

"I should hope so!" Clarence exclaimed.

"Are you and Matt still going to have that little talk?" Joe asked.

"We sure are," Clarence stated. "We've got to clear up this business about Matt wanting to host my show. If Ted Whalen doesn't cancel the show first, I mean."

"Oh, I think Ted might be persuaded to reconsider," Marcy said. "You may not have planned to use that little incident on Tuesday night as a publicity stunt, but it got a lot of attention anyway. And publicity usually means better ratings. And more sponsors. 'The Four O'Clock Scholar' is looking better and better to Ted Whalen now."

"Speaking of Ted Whalen," Frank said, "does he still have orders out to shoot us on sight if he finds us around the studios?"

"Not quite," Marcy said with a laugh. "He's still a little burned up about that last stunt Steve and Debbie pulled with the camera in his office, but he's willing to take into account the fact that you did rescue Clarence and catch a couple of crooks who were using the station as a front for a fencing operation. Even Ted can occasionally be forgiving."

"Well, that's a relief," Joe said. "I'd rather not

make an enemy out of someone who hangs around with big bodyguards who carry guns."

"Before you go, Frank," Marcy added, "I want to remind you that the championship tournament for 'The Four O'Clock Scholar' has been moved to next Sunday. I'll expect to see you and Steve and Debbie right back here in the studios then. And, of course, Joe's always welcome, too."

"Thanks, Marcy," Joe said, as he and Frank stood up to leave. "And we'll look forward to seeing you again, too, Clarence."

"Anytime, old buddy," Clarence said warmly, extending his hand for Frank and Joe to shake. "Anything Clarence can do for you two, don't hesitate to ask."

Outside in the hallway, the brothers spotted a familiar pair walking down the corridor toward them.

"Well, it looks like our friends Steve and Debbie have turned up again," Joe said.

"You know, it's kind of hard to dislike them after they saved our lives," Frank said.

As Steve and Debbie approached them, the Hardys noticed something slightly different about them—they were holding hands.

"Hi, guys," Debbie said.

"How's it going, Frank, Joe?" Steve asked, with a slight touch of shyness in his voice.

"Just fine," Frank said. "You guys look a lot friendlier than the other times we've seen you."

"Yeah," Joe said. "You spent most of the last week trying to bite each other's heads off. Did you call a truce or what?"

"Oh, we never really disliked each other," Debbie said with a smile.

"Nah," Steve said, shrugging. "That's just how we act. You know."

"After we caught those crooks who kidnapped Clarence," Debbie said, "Steve asked me to the dance at school this weekend. I thought that was sweet."

"Uh-huh," Frank said. "Does this mean you're not going to keep trying to prove which of you is the greatest detective any more?"

"Of course not," Debbie said. "We're both great."

"Which is why we're thinking of opening our own detective agency," Steve said. "As soon as we get out of school, of course."

"Uh, there are a few requirements for becoming a detective," Joe said. "Like a license, for one."

"Oh, I'm sure that won't be a problem for a brilliant pair like us," Steve said, grinning. "We'll pass the licensing test with flying colors."

"We're going to call the agency Hertzberg and Burke, Private Detectives," Debbie stated.

"Uh, I thought that was going to be Burke and Hertzberg, Private Detectives," Steve said, looking sideways at Debbie.

"No," she answered, with a firm shake of her

head. "We agreed, remember? Hertzberg and Burke. That has a much nicer ring to it."

"That may be so," Steve said. "But Burke and Hertzberg is alphabetically correct."

"We decided that it was going to be Hertzberg and Burke and that's the way it stays," Debbie retorted.

"You know I'd never dream of contradicting a thing you say," Steve said, "but I will never agree to the name Hertzberg and Burke even if you drive flaming bamboo shoots underneath my fingernails." He began to walk down the hall.

"That's not a bad idea," Debbie said, following him, "and if I were you, I wouldn't put such delightful ideas in my lovely head."

"I couldn't get an idea into your head," Steve said over his shoulder, "if I wedged it in with an ice pick."

Frank and Joe looked at each other. "You know," Frank said, "this could be the start of a beautiful relationship."

"Yeah," Joe said, as he watched Steve and Debbie wander down the hall, bickering all the way. "Or a bad nightmare."

"By the way, we promised to tell Callie and Iola all about this case as soon as it was over," Frank reminded Joe, as they headed for the lobby.

"True," Joe said. "But they've probably read all about it in the newspapers today. There was a big story in the *Bayport Times* this morning."

"Let's call them up, anyway," Frank said. "It's a good excuse to get together, maybe go out to eat. Chet might want to come along, too."

"Chet doesn't *need* an excuse to go out to eat," Joe said.

"Neither do we," Frank said. "I think we've earned a night on the town. Let's get dressed up and do it right."

"Dressed up?" Joe said, looking back toward Studio A. "Hang on a minute. I know where I can get a great deal on some gold chains!"

"Forget it, old buddy," Frank said with a laugh as he grabbed his brother and pulled him out into the parking lot, where they had left their van.

# THE HARDY BOYS® SERIES  By Franklin W. Dixon

# NANCY DREW® MYSTERY STORIES  By Carolyn Keene